BOOKS BY DARRYLE PURCELL IN PAPERBACK

THE HOLLYWOOD COWBOY DETECTIVES SERIES

Mystery at Movie Ranch
Mystery of the Arizona Dragon
Mystery of the Matinee Murders
Mystery of the Alien Banshee
Mystery of the Howling Angels
Mystery of the Horned Monster
Mystery of the Haunted Lion
Mystery of the Hardboiled Hooter
Mystery of the American Yeti

THE MAN OF THE MIST SERIES

(1) Trail of the Bat Beasts
(2) Cave of the Blood Demons
(3) Cauldron of the Hollywood Head Hunters

DARRYLE PURCELL

HOLLYWOOD COWBOY DETECTIVES

MYSTERY OF THE COWBOY SUMMIT

DARRYLE PURCELL

Illustrated

BUCKSKIN EDITIONS

CONTENTS

DEDICATION

Our favorite film cowboys are all wonderful examples of heroes who live by the Code of the West. That means they all fight for what's right, no matter the odds. This book is dedicated to a man I've looked up to all my life. He has always lived by those same good-guy standards: my brother, Lynn Bolton.

CHAPTER 1. COWBOY DIPLOMACY

"I found him!" western film star Hoot Gibson yelled from approximately twenty yards to my right.

I shoved my way through the incredibly tall cornstalks toward his voice. Everything about that morning had been strange but, at that instant, reality took a hard left turn into a bizarre environment littered with unimaginable deadly creatures.

I stepped onto a swath of smashed stalks about the size of a firebreak. Gibson stood not far away, waving his arms to get my attention. I started to run toward him, but slowed down as my eyes focused on what was crumpled on the path near his feet. The bottom half of a man was sticking up out of the ground, sliced apart at his gun belt, with what was left of his intestines strewn across the crushed cornstalks.

"What the hell, Hoot? Is that our man?"

"Yep. The blood trail leads toward the jungle," the cowboy said. "Whatever knocked down these crops dragged the rest of him thataway."

With our pistols held in our right hands, we began following the long smear of blood laced with small chunks of meat. The light of day abandoned us as we passed through a wall of greenery into the thick, damp rainforest jungle. Branches were broken and rocks pushed aside by what we were beginning to expect might be a real nightmare. There were weird prints punched into the mud along the path that certainly gave me the willies.

A little bit earlier, we had been told a story about a ten-foot-long, black, scaly scorpion with the head of a jaguar that hunted cattle and men. At the time, I chuckled at what I considered a typical campfire horror tale to frighten children enough to keep them out of the jungle. But the farther we traveled into the rainforest, the more I began to wonder.

1

An ungodly scream set both of us back onto our butts as a very large reddish howler monkey swung down out of the thick jungle canopy, dropped to the ground next to us and ran toward where we had entered the tangled green ferns, vines and trees.

"Holy crap, Curly! Something really scared that guy!"

"Probably just a coincidence. Howler monkeys all sound like that."

Another scream turned into a roar, just as a large spotted jungle cat raced out of the foliage, leaped over both of us and followed the noisy primate.

"Then again, something may have scared them both."

We jumped to our feet, holding our guns in front of us as we advanced. I watched to the right while Hoot scanned to the left.

"Curly," Gibson said quietly. "You remember that giant scorpion we heard about."

"Yeah."

"I found it."

"Oh, shit!"

"It's dead!"

"Wonderful," I said. "Finally a lucky break."

"Not exactly," he said, looking upward into the thick growth.

I walked over to him and leaned my head back to see what he meant. Nearly fifty feet in the air above us, the ten-foot black scorpion carcass was tangled in a mammoth web, dwarfed by the huge, furry, venomous banana spider that was sucking the fluids from its body. One of the dead creature's claws, broken from its twisted remains, dropped through the branches and crashed to the ground next to us. Then the sucking sound ended as the spider lifted its head and turned eight piercing black eyes down toward us. The red fur of its mouth dripped as the feasting arachnid began an evil clicking sound.

Hoot was first to break free from the beast's hypnotic stare. Then we both raced back toward the corn, doing our best to catch up with and pass the jungle cat and howling monkey, in our attempts to escape with our lives.

Our dystopian odyssey had begun only a few days earlier.

****

MYSTERY OF THE COWBOY SUMMIT

It was the last week of March in 1941, and a rough time for a Republic Pictures flack, or so I thought. I had spent several days at Iverson Ranch with second-unit stuntmen and women, cameramen, directors, cowboys, stock wranglers and hardworking crewmembers who were banging out action scenes for at least three western films. Two of the flicks were upcoming Mesquiteer oaters and the third was an Autry epic. The latter included a Smiley Burnette lookalike stuntman who illustrated his great abilities by falling off a galloping ring-eyed white horse, rolling under a moving wagon and then stumbling onto his face in a mud puddle without garnering a bruise. The man was an artist.

I couldn't wait to see the action on the big screen and the cut to the real Smiley as he struggles to his feet and mugs a stupid expression for the camera. The kids will love it, I thought.

I'm Sean "Curly" Woods, the aforementioned Republic flack. I had been staying at the ranch while, with the help of stills photographer Benny La Rue (no relation to Jack), gathering action shots and behind-the-scenes interviews for promotional articles to be completed prior to scheduled release dates. I made my farewells to the crew and tossed my notes into the backseat of my DeSoto. Benny had promised to deliver his prints to my office by Monday. The best action shots usually came from second unit filming, as the real stars were most often a little too busy at the studio posing for close-ups.

I was really looking forward to getting back to my Culver City bungalow where I could toss all my dusty, stained work shirts and Levis into a bag for delivery to Ding's Two-Day Laundry in Inglewood. Ding was an old friend of mine whose real name was Kevin O'Reilly. I knew him when he was an editorial cartoonist for the *Herald-Express*, before he drew a now-infamous, brilliant cartoon concerning a certain mayor of a large city who was depicted lasciviously assisting a constituent, a lovely but notorious "professional" woman. Following O'Reilly's sudden departure from the paper (the mayor had pull with the publisher), he purchased a local laundry business and adopted the nickname "Ding," after *his* favorite cartoonist, Ding Darling, to use on his new enterprise. "It just seemed right for the business. After all," he said. "Who ever heard of an Irish laundry?"

It was still daylight as I parked and walked up the front steps to my home. I was really looking forward to a nice hot bath. Showers under a movie-ranch water tower near a bunkhouse just didn't cut it. I fumbled with my keys, unlocked the door and entered what I thought would be my nice quiet, peaceful bungalow.

"Howdy, scribe," former western film star and rodeo champion Edmund "Hoot" Gibson said.

"Welcome home, buddy," Republic chauffeur Nick Danby added. "Howzit goin'?"

"What the...?" I sputtered. "How'd you guys get in here?"

I heard the rattling of bottles as my kitchen door was pushed open and G-man Big Jim Webber walked into the living room with four bottles of beer, which he had obviously pilfered from my fridge, clutched in his arms.

"He let us in," Nick answered.

"And the amazing part is," the always-mysterious federal agent added, "that I'm not really here right now."

I tossed my carpetbag of dirty clothes and traveling supplies against the wall, took a beer from Big Jim and sat down to await further explanations.

"By the way, Curly," Jim said. "You either have a couple of extremely rude raccoons camping in your kitchen, or that big yellow cat that growled at me from your windowsill is very unhappy with the available feline services in this establishment. Don't go in there barefooted. I'm just sayin'."

"That damned cat!" My bungalow was probably one of five homes that the yellow peril, whom I had named "Spade" after my favorite pulp detective, considered his property. When I was around, I always fed him halfway decent rancid leftovers. But when I had to be out of town, I just assumed he'd invite himself to one of his other abodes for dinner.

"Jim has already talked to my brother," Nick said. "And we have a rather unique, off-the-books assignment."

"Party time!" Gibson added with his bottle held high.

Nick's brother, Republic Pictures Executive Producer Rick Danby, was my boss. And although my primary job function was the promotion of the studio's signature western films, Nick, Hoot and I had been assigned many "special" jobs over the last few years. Usually, we cleaned up the messes created by a few out-of-control actors. But, once in a while, we had to protect the stars, the studio and/or the industry from various blackguards, including organized crime mobsters, blackmailers and a variety of foreign interests bent on the destruction of all things American.

"What about my publicity features for the Mesquiteers and Gene Autry flicks?"

"Rick can handle 'em, Curly," the mean chauffeur said. "Flacking B-westerns isn't propeller science, you know."

I looked back at Big Jim and waited for the other shoes to start dropping.

"You boys have always been such wonderful helpers whenever you've been involved with national security situations," the smarmy fed said, as if he were about to try to sell us a dusty, used 1939 Crosley convertible propped up on concrete blocks. "And the President is very grateful."

"And...?"

"And he thinks you boys would enjoy a little vacation on the taxpayers' dime."

"What kind of vacation are we talking about, Jim?"

"President Roosevelt has planned a little dude-ranch soirée for a select group of South and Central American business interests and he thinks you boys could help our cause. As you know, American cowboy flickers are extremely popular in a variety of foreign countries. In fact, Hard Hombre Hoot is considered almost godlike in Chile."

"Only Chile?" Gibson asked.

"So what would our involvement encompass?"

"The President thinks you boys would be instrumental in making alliances with some very important international entrepreneurs."

I looked at the silly grins on my inebriated friends and then back at the G-man. "You want *us* to be diplomats?"

"That's one way to put it."

"Jim. Together, we've destroyed National Socialist and Soviet Socialist sabotage basecamps while killing and capturing spies, gangsters, assassins and their corrupt minions. What parts of those activities would you consider diplomatic?"

"The parts I've always made up in my reports to the President that softened the destructive reality of your efforts."

"So Roosevelt thinks we're a bunch of smiling, glad-handing, back-slapping buffoons who tagged along on some of your G-man successes?"

"That's about it," Jim said. "And, you're welcome."

As I saw Hoot and Nick squabbling over the last bottle of beer from my fridge, I looked back at the fed and shook my head. "Diplomacy? What's the matter? Weren't Moe, Larry and Curly available? I don't think any of the three of us even voted for FDR during any of the myriad times he's appeared on the ballot."

"He knows that," Jim said. "And he forgives you."

"How the hell would he know that?" I sputtered.

"That secret's on a need-to-know basis," he answered. "And you don't."

I had a very uncomfortable feeling about Jim's proposal, obviously unshared by my tipsy cohorts.

"Tell me the plan," I said.

"You three Hollywood Cowboy Detectives will attend the function undercover, pretending to be friendly representatives of Tinseltown. Hoot will be an honored guest, who will pose for photos with the foreign delegates while making friends with everyone."

"I can do that," a voice slurred from under a large white western hat.

"And you and Nick will pretend to be yourselves – Nick will be Hoot's chauffeur/valet and you will be his press agent."

The same 10-gallon cowboy hat jiggled in accompaniment to a quiet giggle filtering up through the brim.

"But all three of you will keep your eyes and ears open while using your normal cynical distrust to watch for any questionable behavior."

"You think there may be some enemy wolves in some of those sheep-skin business suits?"

"A few of the countries that are sending representatives are believed to be secretly assisting our enemies. Several specialists who work for the State Department's new Fiscal and Budget Officer, G. Howland Shaw, are going to be negotiating purchasing contracts with some of the foreign manufacturers. We don't want to be blindsided by sending money to a country or business that may be aligned with the bad guys."

I began to better understand our behavioral precepts.

"What about security?"

"I'll have a couple of our men in the neighborhood," Jim answered.

"Any high profile government attendees?"

"The President is keeping that classified at the moment. But you may recognize one or two."

"And Hoot is going to get top billing on the glamor marquee?"

"Since this is going to be a dude ranch experience, the President has selected a couple of other big-name cowboys to join in the back slapping and grinning."

"What?" Gibson sputtered, as he almost fell out of his chair.

"Surely, Hoot, you'll enjoy reuniting with a couple of your old friends," Webber said. "Buck Jones will be there."

Hoot relaxed and smiled. "You're right. I've known Buck for years. It'll be nice to see him."

"And there's this other guy," the big G-man said, and then continued to mumble quietly.

"I didn't quite hear that, Jim," Gibson said.

"Crash Corrigan," the fed spat.

"What the hell? Not him!" Gibson completed his fall from the chair.

CHAPTER 2. FREINDSHIP FLIGHT

"Okay, so we'll do our best to not embarrass anyone at this cowboy summit," I said. "So where are we headed?"

Big Jim pulled a yellow envelope from his jacket pocket and handed it to me. It contained three passports.

"I took the liberty of preparing your traveling papers for you," the fed stated. "You'll love it this time of year in Brazil."

"Wait a minute!" I exclaimed. "This cowboy-themed shindig is in South America? Why couldn't FDR just invite everyone to your federally owned dude ranch in Arizona?"

The three of us had stayed at Patricia Parson's Running P Ranch during what became known as the Dragon caper.

"Because the President wants to show that we can reach out to our friends to the south," Jim said. "Besides, our dude ranch is currently being improved. For a less questionable image, we've changed the name to Circled Wagons Dude Ranch, and it's under a new manager. Miss Parson's been assigned to other duties, elsewhere."

"Too bad," Gibson said. "She was a doll."

"Yeah," I responded. "And thanks to you, she thought I had a wife and three little girls at home."

"All in good harmless fun, Curly," the mean cowboy said. "After all these years, you shouldn't still be holding a grudge."

"Oh, I'm not, buddy! But I'm really looking forward to working with Crash Corrigan again. He certainly has become one of the greatest cowboys in film today."

Gibson grumbled, "I'll bet they've never heard of him in Chile." He pulled his hat back down over his eyes.

"On that note, and since you're out of beer, I will say goodnight," the fed said as he stood up to leave. "Curly, take charge of your soused companions and be ready to hit the trail early. I'll expect the three of you at Mines Field airport at 9 a.m. Nick's studio Packard already contains their luggage. You need to pack enough clothes and supplies for a week. And once the movie star and his chauffeur are sober, make sure everyone brings pistols."

"You think we might need them?"

"Scouts' motto – be prepared."

"And we won't have any trouble carrying our weapons into Brazil?"

"Don't worry. We have everything arranged. Nothing can go wrong."

I shook hands with the cagey federal agent before he vanished into the night.

"You two know where the bedding is stored," I said to my uninvited guests. "Get comfortable."

"I got the couch!" Hoot hollered, as Nick looked sadly at my overstuffed chair.

I went into the kitchen and cleaned up after my traitorous cat. Then I bagged my dirty work clothes and took a hot shower, during which my mind kept questioning how the three of us were going to pretend to be diplomatic. By the time I packed for our trip and was ready for bed, I could hear my two traveling companions snoring in the living room.

****

I surveyed the auditorium knowing full well that I was the sharpest-attired man on the dance floor. My black tuxedo with white tie and tails fit perfectly as I led my dance partner in a masterful bolero. "My name is Woods, Sean Woods," I whispered in her ear. "I understand you are my undercover contact."

I felt her hot breath on my neck as she nuzzled close and said, "Ah, hyuck."

I pulled my head back and looked directly into the face of Clarabelle Cow.

"What the hyuck?"

The sound of a shot reverberated across the dance floor as my bovine dance partner's polka-dot bow flew from the top of her head. Clarabelle grabbed her horns and ran from the room.

"You are next, Senor Woods!" an armed Bucky Bug said as he pushed the front of his sombrero up to reveal his angry expression.

"But I'm not wearing a bow," I responded as I turned and placed one hand behind my back.

"I was a rising star!" the bandolier-wearing insect spouted. "And then the mouse arrived! Promotional flacks like you fawned over the rodent without giving me a single line of publicity!"

"I write about singing cowboys, and you're a beetle."

"I coulda been somebuggy!" he yelled, while pointing his revolver at my face.

I quickly yanked my hand from behind me, while yelling, "Ah, haw!" To my surprise, unfortunately, I was holding a dustpan containing some cat poop. The angry insect smiled and pulled the trigger.

"Up and at 'em, Curly," Nick said as he kicked my bed. "As Snuffy Smith says, time's a-wastin'."

"Please don't quote cartoon characters this early in the morning," I gasped with one eye open, all the while wondering why I never got to dream about Hedy Lamarr.

I shaved without mishap, brushed my teeth and put on clean Levis, a light-blue western shirt, boots and a morning smile that radiated sincerity on the level of a door-to-door vacuum salesman.

"Good morning, sparkles," Gibson said, as he poured me a cup of Colombian humanity. "This'll cure what ails ya."

Nick tossed a slice of burned toast next to my cup. "I found some leftover eggplant Parmesan in your fridge and put it in a dish for Spade."

"I don't have any eggplant Parmesan in my refrigerator," I explained.

"Well, whatever it was," Nick said, "I figured your cat would enjoy it."

After two cups of coffee, I packed my carpetbag, grabbed my Luger plus three extra loaded magazines, leather jacket and white Stetson and stood at the door, ready to hit the trail.

"He's not very talkative this morning," Hoot said.

"That's a *good* thing," Nick added, as he grabbed his chauffeur's cap and walked toward the Republic Packard.

I tossed my bag into the trunk next to my traveling companions' luggage and climbed into the front passenger seat. Hoot was already stretched out in the backseat with his hat over his eyes.

"So, have either of you conspiratorial diplomats any more specific information concerning our assigned endeavors?" I asked, as Nick pulled away from the curb.

"Nope," they answered in unison.

"So we're supposed to take Big Jim's account that this will simply be information gathering during a friendly get-together at a western-themed resort in Brazil?"

"Yep," two voices echoed.

"Obviously, you two think you're going to enjoy yourselves the whole time we're at the summit?"

"Yep."

"And, you're probably hoping there'll be some Betty Grable and Carmen Miranda-type ladies at this South American dude ranch?"

"Yep."

"Can you think of any reason the two of you great communicators were chosen for this job instead of Gary Cooper?"

"Nope."

I decided to shut up and relax for the rest of the drive to the airport.

It wasn't long before we pulled into a parking lot, departed the vehicle with our luggage in hand and walked toward a small but noticeable gaggle of men standing near an open gate. Two members of the group sported tall white western hats while the other three guys stood on presumably flat feet wearing brown suits and fedoras – obviously Buck Jones, Crash Corrigan, Big Jim and two other feds.

"Just put your luggage on the platform," Jim said. "You'll find it when you reach your destination. I'm assuming you buckaroos all know each other."

Jones and Gibson greeted each other like long lost brothers. Nick and I shook hands with Buck and Crash and then turned to the other feds. I had met agents Long and Wagner during the Hardboiled Hooter caper. By their expressions, I assumed they were still a tad ticked off in that someone in our group at that time, whom I won't name, had continued to refer to them as Lum and Abner.

"It's great to see you again, Curly," Corrigan said with a smile. "You too, Nick."

We had spent some time with Ray "Crash" Corrigan during a public relations tour of hospitals and Saturday matinee presentations a couple of years earlier. And, of course, my duties as Republic flack had kept me in touch with him while he was cranking out Three Mesquiteers adventures. Corrigan had recently left Republic and launched a new western-trio series, The Range Busters, with Monogram Pictures.

"I see you brought Hoot," the tall cowboy added. "It's nice of you to take him out of the home now and then."

"Does Monogram charge you for the film wasted every time you fall off your horse?" Gibson spat at the former Mesquiteer.

I stepped between the two men, who have had a long-running feud concerning just about everything.

"If you've checked any theatre marquee, you'll notice I'm still ridin'. What's your excuse? Oh, yeah. You're retired!"

"Gentlemen!" Big Jim exclaimed. "Your jobs are to be friendly, slap backs and grin – not launch a new Civil War!"

"He started it!" Hoot spat.

"Did not!" Crash stated.

"Oh, this is gonna be fun," Nick said with a facetious grin.

"Well, I plan on enjoying myself," Buck Jones said. "The whole idea of a dude ranch summit in Brazil just strikes me as a wonderful way to make friends and have a great time, all the while helping good old Uncle Sam."

"Yeah!" Crash added. "Me too. What he said."

"And on that note," Webber stated, "your transportation awaits."

The G-man led us through the gate and onto the tarmac toward a Douglas B-18. The two-engine bomber was close to 60-feet long with a 90-foot wingspan.

"That thing armed?" I asked.

"It does contain .30-caliber machine guns," Jim noted, "but no ammunition. The Brazilian government frowns on that. Oh, yeah. And no bombs."

"You mean we're not bringing any Hoot Gibson movies?"

Corrigan asked, to an accompanying growl.

Wagner led the way up the portable steps through a door behind the wing. Long canvas bench-like seats lined the inside of both walls. The G-man pointed to the first five seats near the door for Hoot, Buck, Nick, Crash and me. The two feds sat facing us from seats on the other side of the fuselage.

A tarp-covered mound of cargo was hauled into the plane and stacked in front of us on a pallet, surrounded by a thick-rope net. The ground crew placed an odd-looking canvas package next to the cargo, hooked one end of a line to a metal ring on the net and another longer line to a ceiling-area cable that ran the length of the fuselage.

"Make yourselves comfortable," Wagner said. "We'll be landing at various fuel sites along the way."

Big Jim stood in the door and smiled. "You boys will be able to stretch your legs at our secret fuel dumps in Mexico, Venezuela, Colombia and other out of the way runways prior to reaching your destination. The dude ranch is located in the heart of the beautiful green jungle along the majestic Amazon River. Enjoy. I'll be in touch." He turned and left the plane, closing the door behind him.

"There are lidded buckets latched down in the back of the plane," Long said. "In case of emergency, you know what you can use them for. There will be restroom facilities at each of our refueling stops. These five red canisters are filled with water. And Jim made sure each of you glamor boys have your own official Hollywood Cowboy Detectives cup."

I noticed a line of post-Prohibition "Happy Days Are Here Again" drinking mugs next to the water containers.

"Did you bring any cold beer?" Nick asked.

"There's some fried chicken in this cardboard box," Long continued, ignoring Danby's stupid question. "You might want to dig into that before it goes bad. We also have biscuits, jerky and bananas. Bon appétit."

The two big engines came to life with a loud rumble. And, as the bomber began to move onto the runway for takeoff, I felt a cold phantom finger on the back of my neck. Something just didn't seem right. The plane rocked and rumbled its way into the sky above the City of Angels, all the while I was crossing my fingers that I wouldn't immediately be joining that heavenly choir.

The roar of the engines made conversation difficult, which was probably a good thing. And, by having Gibson seated at one end and Corrigan at the other, we avoided any playground rivalry rhetoric. I noticed the two feds, probably used to long flights in military aircraft, had already pulled their hats over their eyes to catch some shuteye. Gibson and Jones talked for a while, but after about 20 minutes Buck reached into his jacket pocket and pulled out a copy of Raymond Chandler's "The Big Sleep." Somehow, that didn't surprise me.

Within moments, Hoot's posture mirrored Buck's, looking a bit like a goofier version of the great cowboy, as he opened a copy of the latest *Man of the Mist* pulp adventure.

I leaned back against rope netting that cushioned the craft's walls and thought about my traveling companions and our situation. I assumed the netting was there to keep people and cargo from slamming against metal during turbulence. Nick had pushed his cap over his eyes in an attempt to sleep, while Crash glared past me at his nemesis, Hoot, as if he were facing off against an "Undersea Kingdom" villain. The former Mesquiteer eventually gave up on frowning and walked to the grub box where he retrieved a drumstick on which to gnaw.

I hadn't been out of the country since The Great War. For me, that time overseas had served as an education, presenting me with a diploma containing a thousand reasons to never again leave the good old red, white and blue. Often, I knew, justice ceased to exist beyond our borders.

"Perhaps," I thought, "I'm just being a mite paranoid." Although, the hair on the back of my neck tingled in a somewhat poorly communicated warning. "What's the matter with me?" my mind continued. "We're on our way to a resort so we can slap backs, drink beer and have a good time while making friends for America." But those neck hairs weren't listening.

Fortunately, I drifted off into a dreamless sleep; subconsciously thankful for the lack of cartoon bugs, armed flappers, piano-playing frogs and the other black and white denizens of my nightmares.

****

14

"We're going down!" a voice screamed in my ear, causing me to leap to my feet.

"What's the matter, Curly?" a calm Hoot Gibson asked. "We're landing to refuel at a fly speck on the map called Rancho Pinto."

I relaxed my panic-stricken expression into an accusatory glare.

"Hey! Don't be such a grump!" the Hooter spouted as if his feelings had been trampled. "I thought you might want to stretch your legs. Next time I won't bother waking you."

Nick, Buck and Crash wore their best poker faces, while the two feds rolled their eyes enough to cause a slight breeze. The plane came to a complete stop near a couple of wooden shacks. Long swung the side door open, letting in a waft of dry, dusty air.

"There's a soda pop machine inside the main building," Wagner said. "And that smaller shed is a three-seat outhouse. We'll be on the ground for 15 minutes, so don't wander off."

"Wander off where?" Gibson asked. "There's nothing out there but dirt and shrubs."

"That's if we're lucky," Wagner answered. "There's been some rebel activity in this valley recently and we don't want to get in the middle of someone else's war. So stretch your legs, grab a bottle of pop and use the latrine."

We deplaned and, knowing the facilities only contained three seats, split into two groups. Nick, Crash and I joined Wagner on a short trek to the pop machine, while Hoot, Buck and Long went to the can. The pilot spoke Spanish to two local men, who then drove an old tanker truck over next to the airplane. I watched as they used a hose to, quickly, refuel our transportation.

Wagner unlocked the soda machine while tossing a buck on the counter. I grabbed a tolerably cool Nehi orange. Then Nick, who had chosen a root beer, and I headed toward the outhouse as Hoot and gang passed going the other direction. "I hope they have peach," Gibson said.

Looking up at the plane, I saw the local men unhook the fuel hose and climb back down to their truck. Obviously our pilot would not need to use the outhouse, as he stood on a wing and relieved himself.

"How rude!" Nick exclaimed.

"I don't know," I said, as the ungodly outhouse smell reached us some 50 feet from the building. "I believe our pilot has been here before. And I think I might just water one of these creosote bushes along the trail, rather than go any farther."

Two desert shrubs were dampened before we turned and walked back to join our traveling companions at the aircraft.

"They had peach!" an overjoyed Hooter exclaimed.

"I would have preferred a beer," a stoic Nick added.

"Everybody back on the plane," Long announced, as Wagner led us up the steps and into the aircraft. "We've got a long way to go."

"The fed is right," I said to Nick. "We have a total of around 6,000 miles to cover as we hop down through Mexico and over into the jungles of Brazil. Cruising speed for a B-18 is a bit over 150 miles per hour. That's close to 40 hours in the air, with at least a half-dozen fuel stops along the way."

"Oh, crap!" Nick said. "That's two full days of flying without a single bottle of cold beer!"

"What?" Gibson exclaimed.

"Simmer down, boys," Wagner said. "Our next stop is at a small village just a tad north of Mexico City. I don't know if it will be cold or not. But there will be beer waiting. Big Jim made sure there would be a two-hour layover so you guys could rinse the miles off you and have a couple of bottles of suds."

"God bless that duplicitous G-man," Nick said. "When do we arrive?"

"Around midnight. Until then, you might want to gnaw on a biscuit."

Long reached into a basket behind his bench seat and pulled out a stack of reading materials. "I thought about you guys, knowing how much you like to improve your minds with great literature. So I bought these for you before we left L.A."

He placed approximately five dollars worth of ten-cent comic books in front of us. I was instantly offended – for about ten seconds. Then I spotted *The Blue Beetle* issue on top. "Ooh! The Blue Beetle!" I pushed Hoot out of the way to get it, as he wrestled Nick over the latest issue of *Superman* while Crash seemed very satisfied to get a copy of *Tom Mix Comics*. I wiped the excited look off my face and returned to my seat under the disapproving gaze from the corner of Buck Jones' eyes. He shook his head and, I believe, tsked twice before he turned back to his Raymond Chandler novel.

Long got a good laugh at our behavior, until he noticed Wagner was engrossed in a *Dick Tracy Feature Book* comic.

****

The next several hours passed painlessly as, between naps, we all caught up on the adventures of a variety of colorfully costumed cartoon characters and visits to the lidded buckets in the rear of the plane. Of note: During a short period of turbulence, I learned the reason those buckets were strapped to the floor. Luckily, I had just snapped a lid closed when the B-18 dropped a couple of hundred feet. I garnered a bump on the noggin, but was able to walk away smelling no worse than I did prior to the loss of elevation.

When I returned to my seat, a smiling Hoot Gibson came back from visiting the cockpit.

"Bob, the pilot, just told me we'll be landing in about 20 minutes," he said. "You should see the instruments up there. Flash Gordon would have to take a class to fly this thing."

"So you're not going to volunteer to spell the pilot for a while?" I asked.

"No way. I don't have enough arms for all the switches and dials I'd have to deal with."

"Good to know," Nick interjected. "Now I won't worry about crashing."

"Hey!"

"Sorry, Hoot," I said. "You have been known to crash a few planes."

"But!" he sputtered. "That's just ... well ... yeah, I have. Nobody's perfect."

"What about you, Buck?" I asked.

I knew Buck Jones, like Hoot, was a bit of a wild man who enjoyed fast cars and air racing. Unlike Gibson, I hadn't heard about Buck crashing.

"If we were in a pinch, I could fly this contraption," Jones said. "But Bob seems to be doing just fine. I just hope, when we arrive, he is given a day to catch up on his sleep."

The pilot began our descent toward the landing field. Within minutes, we all held on to the ropes as the craft bounced twice before smoothing out, to a degree, and rolling to a stop.

As we exited the aircraft, I noticed we had landed on another dirt runway. There were two hangars and an office building at the airport, both of which were in slightly better shape than the outhouse and soda shack at our prior stop. Three open-cockpit biplanes and a rather beat-up de Havilland Dragon Rapide sat idly near the hangars. Over by the office structure, what looked like a horse-drawn paddy wagon stood quietly, silhouetted in the moonlight.

"That's our coach," Wagner stated.

"Looks kinda creepy," Crash said. "You think it'll take us through Borgo Pass?"

As we approached, the driver seemed excited. He stood up and waved at us from the top of the unique manner of conveyance. The closer we got to the wagon, the more excited he became. He started rattling off Spanish and pointing at us.

"He wants his favorite cowboy star to ride up top with him," Long said.

Gibson and Corrigan both smiled and started for the front of the coach. The driver shook his head back and forth and then pointed at Jones. "Si. Si. Senior Buck!"

With smiles quickly fading, Hoot and Crash turned and joined the rest of us as we entered the wagon from the back. A grinning Jones climbed up with the driver, took off his Stetson and waved it like he was grand marshal of a parade. "Oh, well," Gibson said. "He's lucky we're not in Chile."

We had been sitting quietly on the bench seats for approximately fifteen minutes, when the coach came to a halt. We climbed down on the dirt street of a small village lined with closed businesses. All the shops were dark except for a hotel-saloon, which had dim lights glowing from above and below the swinging front doors.

Jones shook hands with the driver and then joined our procession toward liquid refreshments.

"Quite a fan club," Crash said to Buck.

"Seems like a nice guy," Jones responded. "At least he has good taste when it comes to films."

MYSTERY OF THE COWBOY SUMMIT

Gibson pushed the swinging doors wide as we entered the facility like a thirsty gang of cowboys coming off a trail ride. The room contained four round tables with chairs and a twenty-foot bar. Two inebriated customers sat at one table, not quite aware that gringos had invaded their neighborhood, drinking establishment. Another man, with the brim of his sombrero covering his face, stood at the end of the bar facing an empty glass and a half full bottle of Tequila. Dim lighting emanated from a hanging electric chandelier.

I stepped up to the bar with Long, Wagner, Danby and Corrigan to my left and Gibson and Jones on my right. Opening my wallet, I order seven bottles of Two Xs.

The bartender avoided tripping over his mustache as he gathered our drinks and placed them in front of us along with a bottle opener. Nick quickly opened four of the bottles; then slid the lifesaving device down to Hoot, who popped the tops off the other three. Although I couldn't see my new best friend's mouth, I believed he was grinning from ear to ear as he scooped up my three dollars and gave me a stack of what looked like led coins in change.

There was a group sigh as the weary travelers took their first swig of warm beer. Life was good.

"Gringo bass-tards!" a voice exclaimed from behind us.

I noticed Long and Wagner thrust their right hands up under their lapels where they most assuredly kept their shoulder holsters. The rest of us slowly placed one hand each in our jacket pockets.

"Amerry-kawn pigs!" the voice continued.

In one movement, the seven of us turned to face the tipsy, sombrero-wearing, loose-lipped linguist.

He was aiming a rusty revolver in our direction while snarling in his best Leo Carillo impersonation, "You Hollywood foony boys sink you are cowboys! Where are your toy guns and belts now, Yankees?"

An over-acting Gibson pointed at himself and said, "I'm no foony boy?" At the same time, Corrigan looked at him and shrugged. "That's not what I heard."

"You're right, amigo," I said. "We're from wacky old Hollywood and some of us are actors. And, if you would just put

19

that hardware away, I'd be glad to buy you a drink, senior."

"I thin I will just shoot each of you where you stand," he said, as he threw his head back, squinted his eyes and laughed like a Monogram villain.

That was his first mistake, and his last. Seven pistols quickly appeared and, at the very same moment, fired. Our assailant was instantly endowed with a bowling-ball-sized tunnel through his chest. The bug-eyed bartender and the establishment's two other seated customers froze, as our would-be assassin crumpled to the floor.

"Cowboys, 1," Long said. "Diplomacy, 0."

We placed our weapons back in our pockets and shoulder holsters, respectively, and turned back to the bar. "We need to return to the plane, quickly!" Long exclaimed, while we tipped up our beers and emptied them. Nick tossed a five-dollar bill toward the bartender and said, "I'll take a case of Two Xs, to go."

We left the establishment and, since our coach and driver were nowhere to be found, began walking briskly back toward the landing field. Nick, encumbered with a heavy case of beer, did his best to keep up with us. When he had dropped about twenty yards behind, he yelled, "This isn't just for me, you know."

At that time, Hoot and I lagged back to spell him with his burden.

Less than thirty minutes later, we ran onto the runway. The pilot was seated on a wood railing while smoking a cigar.

"Bob!" Wagner hollered. "Get those engines goin'! We gotta get out of here!"

CHAPTER 3. THE HIGH ROAD TO DANGER

Once again southbound, our plane leveled off. I peeked up above my comic book to see Wagner glowering at me.

"Not my fault," I said, defensively. "El bandito started it!"

"Yeah," Hoot added. "Besides, this was only our first visit with the locals. By the time we get to Brazil, we'll have this diplomacy thing mastered."

"We shot too," Long said to his partner. "It was unavoidable."

"I don't think Big Jim will be happy," Wagner grumbled. "And now we'll have to find a different refueling station on our way back."

Nick returned from the cockpit with his case of Two Xs and started handing out beers.

"Did you just deliver a beer to our pilot?" Wagner asked.

"Actually, I gave him two," Nick responded. "I figured I'd save making a second trip up there."

Now, that made sense to me, as I swigged from my bottle of warm Mexican beer. But, from looking at Wagner, I perceived that fed was beginning to get angry. Nick and the cowboys seemed to have also picked up on the G-man's blatantly subtle body language. We all quieted down and either napped or read comic books. Even Long avoided bothering his partner, so as not to set him off.

****

As the hours dragged on, I began to second-guess my decision to embark on the trip. Why was I there? Big Jim never asked us to do anything that didn't involve real danger. The premise of requesting Hoot Gibson, Nick Danby and me to represent the United States of America as grinning friendship ambassadors

21

became more and more ludicrous the farther south we went — Corrigan and Jones maybe, but not us. The idea that we could be diplomats was ridiculous. That ship had sailed when we ventilated the barroom bandito on our second refueling stop.

I could tell that my traveling companions were also reviewing our situation just by their expressions. Their nerves were obviously on edge, as illustrated when Hoot and Crash almost started throwing fists over who would get to read the *Sheena, Queen of the Jungle* comic book first. The G-men kept to themselves, as they knew they would receive the brunt of the blame for the cowboys' growing irritation. Even Buck Jones was beginning to give the feds the stink eye.

We had looked forward to our third fuel stop so we could stretch our legs, get a couple of beers and maybe meet some friendly people. When Wagner opened the door, I saw another dirt landing strip, this time with only one shack. It was an ancient outhouse that I could smell before my feet touched the ground. Several struggling shrubs were watered, as no one bothered to walk to the shack.

We stood around, kicking rocks and grumbling, while an old man wearing tattered overalls drove toward us in what looked to be a 1929 Ford Model-A truck with a fuel tank mounted on the back. It bounced and farted over to our plane and began pumping, hopefully, gas into our aircraft.

"You think maybe the feds are trying to keep our flight secret?" Nick whispered.

"Well, they've certainly plotted out a travel itinerary for us that lacks all vestiges of civilization."

"Huh?" Gibson asked.

"I have a feeling the rest of our fuel stops will make our first two look like New York Municipal Airport," I explained.

And, like all of my negative predictions in life, I was right.

****

After almost two full days of eating dry biscuits and bouncing through the sky, I decided it was time to visit our pilot, Bob. I entered the cockpit and sat down in the copilot seat without saying a word. I was shocked by what I was seeing. We were flying at treetop level over a thick South American jungle.

I gave myself time to think so I could ask my question in a calm manner.

"What the hell, Bob?"

The grinning, cigar-smoking barnstormer gave me a look that reminded me of a newspaper snapshot of Captain Eddy Rickenbacker, and said, "So, Curly. How'd you like the flight so far?"

"Why are we flying so low?" I shouted.

"So the enemy doesn't see us."

"What enemy?"

"Oh, you know, Curly. Bandits. Governments. Just about everybody down there," he calmly explained. "Would you like a beer? I've got my own case under that tarp."

My shocked expression illustrated my thoughts about his answer, but, then again, I hadn't had a beer in several hours. "Thanks," I said, while lifting the tarp off a case that contained at least twenty empties and a few remaining bottles of beer.

I opened one and took a big gulp as I viewed the miles and miles of jungle canopy below us. A thousand questions swirled through my limited studio-flack brain.

"You drank all those?" I asked, while nodding toward the box of empties.

"Yep."

"Yet you never once passed us to visit the lidded buckets in the back of the plane."

"Oh, Curly. If I did that, we would have hit a tree a long time ago."

I didn't say anything, as I waited for his explanation. He pointed to a hose that came up from the floor near his feet. There was a rubber funnel attached at the top.

"Oh."

"Just one of the perks of being the pilot."

He giggled and waggled the wings playfully. At that moment I realized our pilot could have used a couple more dry biscuits and a few less Mexican beers.

He lifted our altitude a tad where I could see a long winding river meandering through the thick rainforest jungle.

"That's the Amazon," he said. "We are getting near your

destination."

"Good. I can't wait to get a bath and a shave. I hope the host ranch has nice accommodations."

"Big Jim said it does," Bob stated. "But you'll have a bit of a hike to get there once you're on the ground."

"Great!"

A small clearing next to the river came into view.

"That's your destination," Bob said, while opening another beer.

My forehead furrowed with about a thousand wrinkles. "I don't see a landing field."

"Oh, the plane's not landing there," he said, showing his toothy grin once more. "Didn't Big Jim tell you?"

My jaw must have passed the rubber funnel as it dropped to the floor.

"You better go back and join your friends now. Agent Wagner will explain."

I swallowed the rest of my beer and rushed back into the cargo bay. There I saw a bug-eyed chauffeur and three cowboys standing in the middle of the plane wearing heavy packs on their backs.

"Come on in, Curly, and put this on," a wickedly smiling Wagner said while holding up one of the packs.

Long walked along the line of frightened Hollywood residents, slapping their packs, tightening their straps and attaching what looked like canvas belts for each of them to the cable that ran the length of the fuselage.

"They're parachutes, Curly!" Nick exclaimed. "The feds are throwing us out of the plane!"

"Nothing to worry about," agent Long explained. "These are the same chutes some of our special soldiers are using in their training. They are perfectly safe."

"I hate Big Jim!" Gibson said.

"Me too!" Corrigan added.

"What'd you do with our hats?" Jones asked.

"Don't worry about them," Long said. "You'll see them again."

"Now boys," Wagner said. "This is the only way to secretly insert you gents into this operation."

"Operation?" Hoot spat. "I thought this was going to be a

party."

"Oh, it is," Long explained. "And the party starts now!"

The agent spun a latch and opened the door. A rush of wind entered the plane with the accompanied engine noise. "You're up front, Curly!" Wagner yelled as he and his co-conspirator saddled me with the chute and hooked up my line to the cable.

"We'll crash into the trees before our chutes open!" I yelled.

"In the next few seconds, Bob will lift us to eight-hundred feet. Keep your knees together and don't try to land standing up!"

I put my hands against the doorframe and looked down as our plane quickly climbed.

"What about you two?" I yelled at the feds.

"We'll see you later," Wagner stated, while shoving something in my shirt pocket.

"Much later," Long added.

"But..."

Wagner put his boot to my back and yelled, "Go!"

Wagner put a boot to my back and yelled, "Go!"

The sky swallowed me. I looked down toward my feet at the wing above me and realized I was upside down. The blast from the propeller threw my chute out and open. I swung back to where I was below the air-filled canopy. The sky above was becoming littered with swinging, swearing cowboys. Then, the ground began to rise to our arrival, quickly.

My body tightened up like a six-day-old loaf of bread. "What did Wagner say about landing?" I thought aloud through my panic, while lifting my legs as if I could avoid hitting the ground. "Oh, yeah! Don't try to land standing up! How the hell could I land standing up?"

I heard a loud "Kafoomf!" as I hit the ground harder than King Kong off the Empire State Building. Then I heard several more Kafoomfs of varying levels.

It took me a moment, but when I did open my eyes, I saw Nick Danby standing over me watching as I slid along the ground on my back. "Hi, Curly. Anything broken?"

"Hi, Nick. Not that I can feel."

"You might want to unlatch your chute," he said, as I was pulled another ten feet. "You're being dragged."

The slight breeze had filled my chute and caused it to pull me along the ground. I grabbed at the straps that held it on and, quickly, let the thing continue on its travels without me.

"Everyone okay?" Jones hollered.

"Fine as frog's fur," Corrigan responded, while rubbing a bump on his head and stumbling in a circle.

I could see Hoot still laying flat over near the riverbank. We all ran to his writhing, complaining body.

"I landed on a big stupid dog!" he said, while struggling to his feet. "That hurt!"

"Not as much as it did the dog," Crash added.

"What the hell kind of dog is that?" Nick asked, while flipping the creature's carcass face up. "Holy crap! That's a rat! A gigantic ratasaurus!"

"It's a capybara," Jones said, "which is a rodent that can grow to the size of an adult German shepherd."

"Well," Gibson said. "I'm glad it's dead. 'Cause if it were still alive, it would be really pissed at me."

"Those critters are found throughout South America, except for

Chile," Jones explained.

"I wish we were in Chile," Hoot said, while slapping the dust off his clothes. "They like me there. This ground is hard. I had hoped to land in the water where it wouldn't hurt as much."

Jones looked at him, then walked to the dead capybara, picked it up and threw it in the river.

"Why'd you do that?"

"Just watch," Buck said.

The water around the dead rodent instantly began to boil with activity, quickly turning a scarlet color. The boiling subsided and the rodent was gone.

"What the hell?" Hoot asked.

"Piranhas," Jones explained. "The Amazon River contains many types of piranhas, some of which love fresh meat. Had you landed in the river, those cold-blooded, sharp-toothed, ever-so-rude fish would have enjoyed a fine Hooter lunch."

"Hey! Look what I found," Corrigan hollered, while opening up a large canvas bag, which was attached to its own parachute. "It looks like the feds sent down our luggage."

"And our hats!" Nick said, as he reached into the green-cloth container and removed his gray chauffeur's cap and my big western chapeau.

Corrigan yanked out his own large white Stetson and placed it on his head. Reaching back, he grabbed Buck's signature good-guy sombrero and tossed it to him. With his arm back in the bag, he shuffled some of the contents around and brought out a crumpled white hat and tossed it toward Gibson. "Sorry, Hoot. It looks like my suitcase fell on your hat."

The Hooter cursed, unfolded his rumpled ten-gallon topper and pulled it onto his head. We all removed our bags from the canvas and then stood and stared at each other.

"Now what do we do?" Nick asked.

I thought a moment, then felt my shirt pocket to see what Wagner had placed there just before he unceremoniously kicked me out of the airplane. I pulled out a small Tom Mix radio premium compass and a torn piece of paper, which contained a scrawled message, "Follow the trail north for around five miles."

"Five miles?" Nick sputtered. "In this jungle?"

"This is the last time I let Big Jim con me into attending one of his parties," Gibson said, while we started our trek into the massive green rainforest.

"Yeah," Corrigan added. "They say Hollywood parties can get out of line. This one's ridiculous, and it hasn't even started yet."

"But President Roosevelt wants us here," Nick said. "What's with that?"

"Yeah," I quipped, "probably because he really does know that none of us have ever voted for him."

"And if George M. Cohan would really 'Rather Be Right,'" Hoot stated, "he'd start singing and dancing dressed as Robert Taft or Thomas Dewey."

"Holy crap! A snake!" Corrigan squealed.

Buck Jones turned to look as it slithered by his boot and vanished into the greenery. "Don't worry about that one," he said. "It's a constrictor. If he was a bit older and twenty feet longer, he could squeeze you to death. Just don't touch any of those frogs."

"You mean these colorful little tree climbers?" Crash asked, holding his hand out toward a little blue amphibian. "They're kinda cute."

"You ever heard of poison dart frogs?" Buck said. "The juice from one of those guys could kill all five of us."

The former Mesquiteer yanked his hand back quickly. "I hate this place!"

The grumbling continued as we advance very slowly to the north. Gigantic tree trunks loomed all around us, with twisted roots that sprung out of the ground arcing up to ten feet above our heads before dropping back into the soil. The almost impenetrable vegetation contained more shades of green than I had ever seen. Tall, umbrella-like trees with thin trunks towered over us, themselves dwarfed by the thick-trunked jungle trees that ascended approximately two hundred feet into the air. All of the greenery was lashed together by a spider-like webbing of vines and garnished with multiple varieties of moss and fungi. Extremely beautiful yellow, white, blue and red flowers complemented the bright green foliage.

There was a constant chattering and rustling of sounds emanating from all around us, including the mulch-covered soil.

"What the heck is that noise?" Corrigan asked.

"Insects. Lizards. Monkeys. Salamanders. Birds. Frogs, bats, cats," Jones answered.

"This jungle is alive!" Nick interrupted.

"That about sums it up," Jones said. "Everything in this rainforest has a reason to exist, if only to be food for something else."

At that moment, Nick jumped to the side, pointing at a lump that had appeared in the leaf-covered mulch near our feet. We watched as the lump moved rapidly along the path like a crazed lawn mole and then dropped flat.

We all looked up at our recently discovered fountain of information, Buck Jones.

"Probably just a big bug," he said. "Could be a beetle, a centipede, a spider, a scorpion...."

"My vote is for beetle," Gibson suggested.

"The soil in a rainforest is extremely rich with nutrients from all of the rotted organic material it contains," the fountain explained. "Bacteria and insects live on the compost; small animals ingest the bugs; bigger animals devour the small ones; and, of course, when they all die, the bugs get their revenge and they all eventually join the vegetation to become rotted organic material."

"Lovely," Nick interjected.

"If you put your faces close to the ground and lift a layer of leaves during the dark of night, you will be able to see a labyrinth of glowing twigs covered in phosphorous created by decomposition," Jones continued. "Place your ears to the ground, and you can hear the sounds of insects continually enjoying their mulch meal. Sometimes it sounds like the breathing of a giant snake."

"That's about enough, Buck," I said. "Let's just keep going and hope we don't get eaten by this jungle."

"Oh," he said. "The beautiful flowers aren't exactly what you would think either. Many are startlingly colorful orchids. But if you look closely at some of them, you will see that they aren't really flowers after all. Some, like that one over there that looks like a large pair of red lips, are carnivorous."

I started herding the cowboys. "Step lively. Move along. We need to arrive at whatever our destination is before nightfall!"

We continued battling our way north while all of our eyes

scanned the environment for slimy, venomous, carnivorous phantoms in the ferns. I leaned close to Jones and asked, "How do you know all this stuff?"

"I served in the Philippines during the Moro Revolution," he whispered. "There's a lot of jungle there, too."

"And that's where you learned about snakes, bugs, frogs and things?"

"Over the years, I've tried to learn about all kinds of things that might be detrimental to my continued existence," he said. "In the Philippines, I also learned that the civilized rules of engagement meant nothing to the Moro Moslem fanatics. They have about as much respect for anyone who isn't one of them as one of those carnivorous plants has for an insect that stumbles into its trap."

"That war's been over for a long time."

"The shooting has," he said. "But that doesn't mean the enemy has changed its mind."

"So your foreign policy views are about as diplomatic as ours," I stated.

"Maybe less. One of those Moro maniacs shot me."

In my experience, nothing is more successful in replacing the naiveté of youth with common sense values as military combat experience. Gibson and I received our education in France during The Great War. Jones survived his classes more than a decade earlier in the Philippines.

People who haven't experienced the life and death struggles of an international military conflict, very seldom understand a veteran's viewpoint. They would deem Jones' remarks considering the Moro rebels to be "simplistic." These are the same folks who, even post-Chamberlain, seek "Peace For Our Time" by "negotiating" away other people's freedoms and, eventually, lives.

Jones knew the enemies of freedom are not honorable people. They can never be negotiated with for anything. They will make their lies sound acceptable to the gullible, only to strike when least expected – like the rattlesnakes they are.

"You're fully aware that some of the folks who are scheduled to attend FDR's little Amazon clambake are probably agents of America's enemies?" I asked.

"Yep. And I'll give the same trust and consideration to any

supporter of Germany's National Socialists, Stalin's Soviet Socialists, or Hirohito's Imperial murders that I currently have for that," Jones said, while pointing toward the largest, hairiest black spider I had ever seen.

The creature, which was posing in the center of a huge white web strung in our path a dozen feet in front of us, was not quite as large as the rodent that Hoot killed.

All five of us stood motionless as we considered our options. I believe we each, independently, came to the same conclusion that running, screaming into the jungle wasn't our best move.

"How do we get around him?" Gibson asked.

"He is probably a she," *Professor* Jones explained. "And, at that size, I'll bet she has devoured a good number of her clueless ex-husbands."

"I'll rephrase my question," a slightly perturbed Hoot said while showing a lack of patience. "How do we get around Helen, or Sally, or whatever her name is?"

Buck placed his carpetbag on the ground, reached into his jacket pocket, pulled out a revolver and smiled. "No problem."

The .38-caliber hollow point slug hit dead center, causing the late widow spider to thrash her hairy legs wildly, tangling her corpse in her own sticky net trap.

I tossed a couple of broken branches against one side of the web, giving us enough room to get around it. Warily, we continued our hike.

"They sure make things big in this jungle," Nick said.

"You ain't just woofin'," Hoot stated, while pointing to a pile of dirt and leaves just off our path.

I walked over to what looked like a recently constructed ridge of loose soil. With the help of a branch walking stick, I climbed to the lip of the dirt-clod mound and looked down into a very big, deep hole. My traveling companions joined me as we surveyed the unique ground formation.

"What the hell do you think rolled up out of that?" Corrigan spat.

"Although it would fit," Gibson said, "I don't believe it was a Helms Bakery delivery truck."

"Okay!" I offered. "We need to get a move on! We have to have covered close to five miles by now. Our destination should be just ahead!"

"I hope we can find someone soon!" Nick added.

"Not to worry," Jones offered. "Someone found us."

Close to a half-dozen rifle barrels protruded from the jungle foliage around us – all pointing in our direction.

CHAPTER 4. EL RANCHO GRANDE

We stood quite still as the Springfield M-1903 rifles moved closer, followed by a ragtag group of men in tan uniforms and unhappy expressions. They wore western hats, pistols on their hips, grenades on their belts and knives attached to their boots.

"They look like well-armed cowboys," Crash said.

"Gauchos," Gibson corrected.

"Actually, this far north, they're vaqueros," said Jones, whose knowledge of just about everything was beginning to irritate me.

Two of the armed men began to chatter in what had to be Portuguese. They walked up close to Crash Corrigan and pointed at him. "Senhor Mesquiteer!" The Monogram ham began to smile and nod. Then another vaquero's eyes bugged out with recognition as he shouted. "Buck!"

I began to relax, thinking we had run into a contingent of western film fans. Gibson walked over to a couple of the excited men, tipped his Stetson to the side of his head and gave them a big Hooter smile. The men looked closely at him, furrowed their brows and thought. One leaned and whispered to his friend, who then shook his head from side to side. The whisperer looked confused, then quietly asked Hoot, "Frog Millhouse?"

Gibson puffed up like a toad, shoved his hands into his pockets and said, "Obviously, these men have never been to Chile."

One of the men motioned for us to follow, as the Springfield rifles were casually pointed toward the ground. For Brazilian cowboys those guys seemed a smidge over armed. Then again, I thought, we might run into another spider.

I'm sure, we were all hoping our vaquero entourage was leading us to our party house destination. I was getting rather tired and personally would have been overjoyed to see a nice Gene Autry-style hacienda, a neighborhood bar, an airplane hangar or even a Harvey House. What I wasn't expecting was a massive concrete wall. A fifty-foot firebreak had been cleared out of the jungle in front of the barrier, which seemed to go for miles in both directions.

We hiked alongside the wall for another hundred yards or so before arriving at a large metal door. The mustached leader of our new "friends" spoke into a small grill-covered box, which I assumed held a microphone, inset into the concrete next to the closed entryway. He turned toward us, smiled and put up his hands to his sides as if to say, "Relax. Everything is fine." Or he could have been informing us, "Now, we will kill you." I'm really not very good at deciphering body language. I remember this blonde I met at the Trocadero, and…. But that's another story.

The sound of a heavy bolt being lifted preceded the metal door's slightly inward swing. The five of us entered to face a heavyset man in a dark suit, who slammed the gate behind us, leaving the vaqueros on the outside. Wherever we were, the facility we faced was immense. Any of Father Serra's California missions would have been dwarfed by the size of the tile-roofed Spanish mansion in front of us. We stood on a brick patio area that led to an arched enclosure, which was large enough to hold a Benny Goodman concert. Our doorman simply pointed toward the covered area. Inside the overhang I could see a tall man silhouetted in the shadows.

"Maybe that guy speaks English," Gibson said.

"I hope so," Crash commented. "I'm ready for a room and a bath."

"And a beer," Nick added.

Buck advanced toward the silhouette with his right hand out. "Hello. I'm Buck Jones. My friends and I are hoping you speak English."

The tall, redheaded man wearing a black tuxedo stepped out of the shadows and shook the western star's hand. "I do. And it's nice to finally meet you, Buck. I'm Slate. Donovan Slate."

The rest of us smiled, walked up and started slapping backs. We all knew the tall G-man with the big grin. Slate, Big Jim's right-hand man, was a real pal who had worked with us on many dangerous assignments over the years.

"It's good to see a friendly face!" Gibson said.

"What kind of place is this?" I asked.

"Where's the beer?" Nick cut to the chase.

"I'm glad you guys are here," Slate said. "How was your flight?"

Five smiles immediately reversed themselves.

"How was yours?" Gibson sputtered. "You didn't hit the ground in that monkey suit, did you?"

"Actually, I just got here this morning," Donovan responded. "And I wore slacks and a Hawaiian shirt on the flight. This outfit was in my carry-on bag. Most of my luggage is still on our plane at the ranch landing field."

"Landing field!" I spat.

"The boys and I came in with the budget specialists. You cowboys are pretty much the last 'diplomats' expected to arrive."

"Is Big Jim here?" I asked harshly. "Because if he is, I'm gonna take him back through that metal door and introduce him to a spider!"

"He's not here," Donovan answered, "but he did tell me to thank you guys for droppin' in."

"I'm gonna kill him!" Gibson exclaimed.

"Calm down, Hoot," Donovan explained. "This way, we'll get you guys cleaned up and, when you join the party, it's gonna be a real surprise to all your South American fans."

Gibson and Corrigan looked at each other a moment, while Buck just shook his head as if he thought we were all insane.

"Besides your attendance being a secret, your unique arrival allowed you to bring your personal weapons with you," Slate continued. "If you had flown along with us, you wouldn't have made it through Mexico City's airport security checks, let alone our stops in Panama, Bogota or any of the other cities."

"You landed in big cities?" Nick asked. "Big cities that have beer?"

"Well, yeah. But we're the official delegation. You cowboys are the secret diplomats. Oh, and President Roosevelt says 'Thank you.'"

Gibson and Danby responded with a wet-sounding, harmonized strawberry.

"Let's get you guys to your rooms so you can get cleaned up," Slate said, as he quickly turned to lead the way into the monolithic structure.

As we followed Slate into the enormous hacienda, Nick and Hoot's grumbling masked the sounds of the mechanical gears spinning in my head. I knew that Big Jim had a twisted sense of humor. But I was sure that our less-than-first-class travel arrangements had to have been more than just a gigantic Rooseveltian practical joke. I hoped. I gave the devious fed the benefit of the doubt, temporarily, while deciding to keep an open mind.

Once inside, we followed a long hallway that contained many doors along the sides, both open and closed. I saw an auditorium-sized pantry through one opening and a large warehouse in another. At the end of the hall, we entered into a busy kitchen filled with chefs, helpers and tuxedo-clad waiters, all moving about with their chores while babbling at each other in what I assumed was mostly Portuguese.

"Supper is being served in the formal dining area," Slate said. "But don't worry. I've had sandwiches and beer sent to your rooms. Once you guys get cleaned up, I'll give you a rundown on some of the people you will be meeting. Just stay relaxed. Nothing can go wrong."

I glowered at the fed. "I believe Big Jim said that just before we left L.A."

"And, you all made it here safe and sound," Slate said. "Everything's fine. Trust me."

Following a communal double take, three groans, a choke and one possible spit, the straight-faced G-man led us out of the kitchen and up a circular stone stairway. "Our apartments are on the third floor."

We exited the stairs onto a catwalk style walkway overlooking a large open courtyard filled with stone-framed gardens, picnic tables and tile floors that allowed areas for decorative trees and shrubs; all surrounding a center-point statue of what looked like a scale-covered grizzly bear with a beaver tail. Water flowed downward from the stone beast's fang-filled open mouth into a small pond at its feet.

"How delightful," Nick stated.

"The next three rooms are ours," Slate said. "Hoot, you and Nick are in the first room. Buck and Crash will occupy the second.

Curly, you'll be bunking with me in the third."

The rooms were identical with tile floors and stone-covered walls. Each contained two beds with end tables, a couch, a wooden table with chairs, a large oak armoire, an electric refrigerator containing sandwiches and cold bottles of Mexican beer, potted shrubs, and a private bathroom with tub and shower.

****

Following a very refreshing shower, I donned a comfortable white robe that hung next to the sink. There I found a new toothbrush, tooth powder, a safety razor and a shaving stick and brush. Once I was clean, shiny and lacking rainforest odors, I stepped back into the apartment where I found Slate removing a tuxedo from the armoire.

"I took the liberty of making sure all of you Jungle Jims have formal attire," he said.

"If you ever get tired of bein' a fed, you could start a new career as Rudy Vallée's valet."

He also handed me a sleek-looking leather shoulder holster.

"This was custom-made for your favorite handgun," he said. "It's undetectable under your formal jacket."

I picked up my Luger from one of the end tables and slid it into its new holster. "That's real nice. And I assume the cowboys all received appropriate versions for their firearms choices."

"Yep. We don't want them to look like Monogram gunslingers. But we also understand that you guys need quick access to firepower."

The G-man's tux jacket didn't have any tell-tail bulges, yet when he opened it, he revealed a snug leather holster with his choice high-caliber cannon.

"Expecting trouble?"

"Scouts' motto. Be prepared. We have a leather craftsman in D.C. who is a real artist."

It didn't take long for me to don my formal attire, shiny shoes and funny little tie. As I stood in front of a floor-length mirror, while buttoning my jacket, the door opened and a parade of tuxedo-clad clodhoppers traipsed into the room. The three cowboys all sported black boots and their big white Stetsons.

Nick, hatless and wearing shoes like mine, walked in and slapped me on the back.

"At least two of us will look like we belong at a cocktail party instead of a hoedown," he said.

"Make that three," Slate added. "But we also *want* our cowboy celebrities to stand out, while the rest of us just blend in."

"Mission accomplished," Gibson said. "We look about as western in these outfits as Calvin Coolidge did while wearing a passel of Sioux Indian feathers on his head."

"Don't be so hard on yourself, Hoot," Nick offered. "You look majestic enough in that monkey suit that, perhaps, Crash could get you a spot in The Range Busters as a stand-in for Max Terhune."

"Enough, boys!" Slate exclaimed. "Sit down. The sooner we get this show on the road, the sooner you guys can go downstairs and join the party."

Nick and I landed on the couch. Buck and Crash pulled chairs from the table while Hoot leaned back on one of the beds. Donovan continued to stand as he began his presentation.

"You're going to be meeting movers and shakers from all over South and Central America. You cowboys will slap backs, give autographs and try to figure out whether your new fans are friends or foes. Nick, I want you and Curly to concentrate on the foreign dignitaries' support staff."

"That's because we're not celebrities," Danby said, while sticking out a pouting lower lip.

"That's okay, Nick," Crash said. "We'll treat you almost as well as if you were as good as us."

"Yeah," Hoot agreed.

"*And* I'll continue," said a very tolerant Donovan Slate. "The owner of Rancho Grandé, which is this outlandishly large hacienda and thousand-plus acres compound, is Dom Sebastian. As kind of a recluse who stays mostly in his private offices, he is very seldom seen. His sister Maria, however, is our hostess."

"Is she pretty?" Nick asked.

"Maria has been instrumental in gathering our State Department personnel, as well as representatives of Latin manufacturing, agricultural, mining and other interests that may be of use to America, if war were to be declared."

"You're sayin' the Lend Lease Act may be expanded to serve more than just England," I said.

"Exactly. For the time being, we, the U.S., need all the assistance we can gather to help keep the rest of Europe, Africa and Asia from being enslaved."

"Okay," Gibson stated, "so who else besides Maria will we be socializing with?"

"And is she pretty?" Nick never gives up.

"Yes!" Donovan seemed a bit touchy. "You'll also meet with Rancho Grandé foreman Esteban Garcia and Dr. Anita LaFond, who is a botanist. She has been at this compound for the last few years experimenting with methods of enhancing crops for a more stable world food supply."

"Is *she* pretty?"

"Curly! Is there anything you can do about him?"

"No, Donovan. We've tried."

"Our federal acquisitions negotiators are," Slate sputtered as his complexion began to match his hair color, "Arlis Unger, William 'Bill' Hunziger, Penrod Little and Arlene Mistevin." Nick started to raise his hand, when Slate thrust his face in front of him. "And, yes, she's pretty too!"

"So what are we waiting for?" Nick asked.

"I have one question," I said. "I assume there is a reason why we armed but unofficial detectives are here rather than more real honest to goodness diplomats and/or G-men. Therefore, what is it you are not telling us, Donovan?"

The G-man momentarily adopted an expression of shocked innocence. Then, realizing it wasn't working, answered, "Depending on what you boys uncover, we will have to deal with the situations in a rather off-the-books manner. Federal agents cannot engage in behavior that might just send possibly friendly governments toward the other side."

"So us expendable clodhoppers might just have to get into a little fracas with a few communist, National Socialist and/or fascist black hats," Jones said. "And that way you feds can just shrug your shoulders and say, 'What do you expect out of a pack of Hollywood crackpots?'"

"Well, that's putting it a bit rough, Buck," Slate said. "But, yeah! And then again, you might just have a good time for the next few days. After all, there are a few very pretty ladies involved."

Frowning Hoot, Crash and Buck formed a circle around Slate.

"Easy, boys," I said. "We all know that when Big Jim invites us to attend a party, we're liable to end up in Berlin wearing snorkels while dogpaddling in Martin Bormann's punchbowl. Let's just go downstairs, mingle, have a few more beers and check out those good-lookin' gals."

"I'm with you, Curly," Nick added.

****

Slate led the way toward our grand entrance to the party. We took the stairs to the first floor where we then began our long march down one of the mansion's many hallways. Buck started to say something, when an apartment door opened and a young lady stepped out in front of us. We froze in our tracks, dropped our jaws and stared at her like a pack of really stupid wolves.

She had curly blonde hair, red lips and blue eyes that harmonized with her delightful giggle as she saw the six of us gaping goofballs standing in the hall. Her shimmery silver gown clung to her amazing figure almost as tightly as I would have, given the chance. With a smile that made me forget to breathe, the tall, slender vision of Heaven closed the door to her room and said, "Hello, Donovan. I see you brought your posse."

"Hey, Misty," Slate said. "These yahoos are Nick, Curly, Buck, Crash and Hoot."

"Sounds like a law firm of former professional wrestlers."

"Boys, meet Arlene Mistevin."

"Call me Misty," she said, as she hooked her left arm through my right. "We better get a wiggle on. I'm dyin' for a beer."

My complexion glowed red enough that, if I were in Chicago on a foggy day, I could have brightened the path of the Montgomery Ward Santa float during the Christmas parade. My Hollywood pals seemed to vanish as Misty and I glided arm in arm toward our destination, wherever that was. I found it amazing that we were actually moving, in that my feet never touched the floor.

At the end of the hall, the G-man pushed a large oak door

inward, exposing the very crowded and noisy courtyard. Misty and I entered the party with whomever those other guys were wearing the white hats following. Somewhere to the right, an orchestra was banging away with a rather unique but somewhat familiar sound. The piano jolted me to my recognition of Hoagy Carmichael's amazing "Stardust," presented with a Latin beat.

"It sounds like Carmichael and Cugat engaged in a bar fight," Misty said, while pulling me toward a small bar next to a potted rubber tree. She pointed out her order and a smiling bartended handed each of us a bottle labeled "XX."

"Nectar of the gods," she said, while sipping like a kitten.

"You should know," I said, thinking I was being clever. Unfortunately, when I lifted my bottle to take a drink, I missed my mouth.

I felt a slight breeze, as Misty batted her beautiful eyelashes and put a finger up to my lips. "There's your target, Curly. Try again."

"I never thought I'd see the day that my elderly pal Curly needs directions on how to drink a beer," the rude chauffeur said. "Hi, Misty. I'm Nick."

My former friend grinned like a hyena while crowding between us to order a brew.

"Oh, yes, Mr. Danby," she said. "Donovan told me all about you guys. You're the little man who gets to drive all those big important movie stars around."

"Haw!" My delighted response sent a fine spray of two Xs onto Nick's deflated expression.

The friendly bartender chuckled, held out a bottle to Nick and said in his best doctor-patient voice, "Take a gulp of this, young man. It should help."

The lovely Misty took my arm again and we walked back toward the music.

"He deserved that," she said.

"And more!" I added, with a smile

The large courtyard was as congested with international celebrants as a formally attired snake pit. I saw Buck and Crash laughing and conversing with a fun crowd of smiling men and women. Hoot was sipping a beer, alone, leaning up against a short, smooth Tuscan column that supported a potted fern.

Then I saw a surprising sight. A weasel-like man with greasy slick hair laughed with his hand on the shoulder of an Argentine military officer.

"Isn't that U.S. Sen. Ted Bilbo, Democrat of Mississippi?" I asked.

"He does stand out, doesn't he?"

"What the heck is he doin' here?"

"Probably trying to get a good deal on cotton sheets for his favorite hometown fraternal association."

"Who's that with him?"

"I don't know the uniformed goose stepper, but the short, stocky guy is Bill Hunziger."

"Isn't he one of you...?"

"Yeah. But, you remember Will Rogers saying he 'never met a man he didn't like?'"

"Uh, huh."

"Well, Hunziger has never met a powerful politician he didn't like."

Misty and I sat down on a stone bench next to a palm tree.

"So, Misty," I stuttered, and asked the obvious. "What do you do for the State Department?"

"I'm here to investigate the viability of importing food that could be used for our military and aid packages."

"Doesn't Roosevelt think American farmers could fill the bill?"

"Our farmers can handle a lot of our needs," she said. "I ought to know. I grew up on a cattle ranch in Texas."

"Then why make deals with foreigners?"

"As you are certainly aware, we are on the brink of another world war. And, I'm sure you remember from the first one, with that comes an immediate need to keep our military supplied, as well as our aid to allies. War leads to massive refugee camps. Hunger will probably kill more civilians than bombs. We need to be ready."

"That makes sense. Even though I'm surprised we haven't already been dragged full force into Europe and Asia's killing contests, I'm like everyone else. I don't like to think about it."

I couldn't in good taste tell her what I was really thinking about.

"We have to prepare, Curly. And making sure we have enough

food for our troops and friends is just as important as having enough ammunition to take on our enemies."

"So you're here to talk to representatives of ranching, farming and canning businesses?"

"Nope. I'm here to take a look at an alleged scientific wonder right here at Rancho Grandé. And on that note..." she stood up, as I practically needed a crowbar to pry my eyes away from my new favorite State Department employee.

A very dignified couple walked up to face us. The man, who was probably in his early fifties, had thick white hair with a pencil-thin mustache to match, and was wearing a black tailless tuxedo with a red cummerbund, and black riding boots. His lady companion wore a floor-length black gown that enhanced her delightful curves and long, wavy raven-black hair. Her age could have been mid-thirties.

"Are you enjoying yourself, Misty?" the sultry brunette asked with a very slight accent.

"I'm just getting started," the angelic blonde said. "This is my new friend, Curly Woods of Hollywood. Curly, I'd like you to meet our hosts, Dom Sebastian and his sister, Maria."

I shook hands with the gentleman and then grasped Maria's hand and said, "I am honored. From what I've seen so far, you have an amazing home."

Maria smiled and stated, "As your Mr. Jolson likes to say, 'You ain't seen nothin' yet!'"

"It's very nice to meet you both," Dom Sebastian said. Then he turned to his sister. "I must get back to work."

"My brother very seldom leaves his office," Maria said. "He just spent ten minutes meeting a few of our guests, and that's the longest he has ever socialized in a large group like this."

"And we are pleased we were able have our moment," Misty said. "I was just telling Curly that I am at Rancho Grandé to see a scientific wonder."

"And so you shall," our hostess said. "Mr. Woods, I understand you work for Republic Pictures."

"I do."

"Then you can ride?"

"Well, I'm no Ken Maynard," I said. "But I'm pretty good in the saddle."

"Good. Tomorrow morning I'd like to show you and Misty around some of our property. I think you will be amazed."

"'Lookin' forward to it."

"I'll have our ranch foreman, Esteban Garcia, meet you at this bench at 9 a.m. He will escort you to our stables," she said. "Oh, and you don't need to wear that monkey suit anymore."

"Thank God," I said, as our hostess turned and vanished into the crowd.

Misty took my hand and led me up near the orchestra to where several couples were dancing. The band was playing "Red Sails in the Sunset."

"Enough of the trivialities of our assignments," I said. "Let's get down to the most serious issues, such as, are you seeing anyone?"

"I'm lookin' right at you."

"Let's dance."

For the next hour we held on tightly and stared into each other's eyes, while gliding across the floor in a manner that would have made Fred and Ginger jealous. Or at least that was my perception.

"You really like to dance, don't you, Curly?"

"The music just moved me along."

"That doesn't explain the time during the band's ten-minute break."

"As long as I look into your eyes, the music plays."

I felt a tap on my shoulder.

"Scram, bub. No cutting in."

I felt it again. And I turned angrily to face… Donovan Slate.

"Sorry to interrupt, Curly. But I need your help with one of your brother diplomats."

"What did Hoot do now?"

Slate smiled and pointed toward a large group of laughing men and women. "Hoot's doin' fine. He's over there with Arlis Unger and a contingent of Chilean representatives."

Then he pointed toward a gaggle of people standing around a knocked over palm tree.

"It's Nick. He's had a few too many beers and got himself into a little scuffle with one of our State Department officials. Penrod Little."

I pulled Misty back into my arms. "Nothing to worry about, Donovan. Nick can handle himself. Especially against some pencil pusher with the name Penrod."

"Um, Curly," Misty whispered. "Penrod ain't so little."

I looked back toward the area of altercation and saw a big-eyed Nick Danby quickly sobering up several feet off the tile floor. A baldheaded tuxedo-wearing Goliath used his left paw to hold the little chauffeur up by the back of his collar, while pulling his right bowling ball-sized fist back in preparation to knock him into next week. I ran toward the possibly terminal situation.

A baldheaded tuxedo-wearing Goliath used his left paw to hold the little chauffeur up by the back of his collar, while pulling his right bowling ball-sized fist back in preparation to knock him into next week.

"Hang on there, Mr. Little!" I hollered. "Don't kill him!"

The big fella turned his glowering expression toward me.

"Just who the hell are you?" he growled.

"I'm his boss," I said, with my hands on my hips. "Just what did he do?"

"This squeak made fun of my name!" Little lifted the chauffeur higher.

"Oh, for Heaven's sake, Nicholas Danby! Did you do that?"

Nick spread his arms, hands forward, and said in a somewhat Stan Laurel voice, "Gee, Mr. Woods. I guess I might have misspoke."

"Mr. Little. I apologize for my irritating, smartass chauffeur," I said. "I do hope he has learned a lesson here, and that you will forgive the drunken little turd. I guarantee it won't happen again."

A sad-eyed Nick looked at Penrod Little with the expression of an almost drowned kitten.

"Well, I don't know…"

"And if you could just put him down," I added.

The big man released Nick's collar, dropping him to the tile floor.

"You probably should have said 'gently,'" Donovan whispered.

I helped Danby to his feet. "Come along, Nicholas. When we get you back to your room, I will give you a stern talking to." Then I added, "Good night, Mr. Little."

Donovan and I escorted Nick to the hall entry.

"Where's Misty?"

"Oh, she left," Slate explained. "She told me to tell you 'good night,' and that she would see you in the morning."

I turned toward Nick with my angry expression. "Thanks a lot, buddy."

"Hey. You didn't need to butt in. A had that Palooka right where I wanted him."

CHAPTER 5. CURLY IN WONDERLAND

"Up and at 'em, Curly," Donovan said in his best fingernails on the chalkboard voice. "You need to get ready to hit the trail."

"Umphg!" I responded in kind.

"Open your eyes and meet the day. There's coffee and toast waiting for your ascension."

"Flgroomph!"

"It's 8:15 in the morning," Slate stated. "Aren't you going riding with someone at 9?"

My eyes popped open. I jumped to my feet. "Where the hell's that coffee?"

It usually takes two or three large mugs of java to get all my cylinders firing properly. I finished my last cup and jumped into the shower. Within twenty minutes, I was clean, shiny and ready to ride the Rancho Grandé fences with marvelous Misty. I felt quite comfortable in western boots, a yellow bandana, Levis, a light-blue Gene Autry-style shirt and my big white Stetson. "Yeehaw!" I held my jacket thrown over my left shoulder, with my Luger in one of the pockets.

I hurried downstairs and to the courtyard, which looked even larger without all the formally attired celebrants from the night before. My boot heels clicked on the tiles as I rushed toward the stone bench by the palm tree. Then I saw the most beautiful cowgirl north, south, east and west of the Pecos. A black Bill Hickok hat sat cocked to one side on her lush curly blonde hair, which framed the bright blue eyes and red lips that smiled in my direction. She wore an orange bandana, light blue shirt, snug jodhpurs and slick riding boots.

"Good morning, Curly. I see you were able to rescue your friend without getting bruised up."

"Piece of cake. You look lovely."

49

"It's a beautiful morning. I'm looking forward to a nice ride."

A tall man, wearing the same outfit as the vaqueros that greeted us in the jungle, walked up to us and smiled. He had a holstered Luger strapped, gunfighter style, to his leg.

"Bom dia. Good morning, my friends," he sputtered through his thick graying mustache. "I am Esteban Garcia. Are you ready for a morning ride on the rancho?"

"Howdy, Esteban," I said. "We're ready to go."

The man seemed friendly enough. Jolly, in fact, in a rather forced manner. I assumed the ranch honcho was just a bit uncomfortable having to deal with a couple of gringo visitors.

We followed the foreman out of the patio and along a gravel walkway lined by white wooden horse fences toward a warehouse-size, red barn. Hitched in front of the structure stood five saddled horses of varying shades of brown and gray. The only thing they all had in common was what could only be described as an equine version of the Barrymore nose.

Standing next to the mounts were Maria and, surprisingly, Hoot. Gibson was wearing his usual big hat, yellow bandana, Levis, boots and a colorful western shirt that would only have sold well on Hollywood Boulevard or at the Braille Institute gift shop. He also was wearing a six-shooter on his hip, probably in case he had to face off against another spider. Maria was dressed in black boots, jodhpurs, blouse and small derby-like riding cap. She broke up her dark theme with an orange scarf.

Another rather dignified looking gentleman could be seen in the shadows of the barn door. At an inch or two above six feet, the sandy haired man wore khakis, a dark blue shirt, Levis, black riding boots and a pencil-thin mustache on his stiff upper lip. He kept both eyes on Maria, as if waiting for instructions.

"Those are some mighty majestic horses," I said, as we greeted one another.

"All of our horses are Brazilian," she said. "Campolinas."

"Well, that one standing next to Hoot looks like he's ready to do a scene from Hamlet," I said.

"You may have noticed our horse trainer, Dante," she said, motioning toward the man in the doorway. "He has done wonders with our stock."

The man in the shadows snapped his heels together and

nodded toward the lady in black.

"I asked Mr. Gibson to join us this morning," Maria added. "As a well-known rodeo champion, I wanted to get his opinion of our stock."

"I can tell you right now, these are some fine-lookin' mounts," Gibson offered.

Esteban was the first to mount up. His saddle included a rifle scabbard containing a Springfield M-1903. I thought about my Luger and decided, for safety purposes, I'd best wear my jacket rather than carry it. The foreman led our tour with Maria and Hoot next and Misty and me bringing up the rear.

"Rancho Grandé includes more than one thousand acres," our hostess said. "If you will look to our left, you will see a large brick structure attached to a glass greenhouse. That is where a lot of our plant-life research takes place. Following this morning's tour, I will take you there and introduce you to Dr. Anita LaFond, our research scientist. She and her crew are responsible for some of what I am about to show you."

"So a woman scientist is responsible for the 'scientific wonder' you've mentioned?" Misty asked.

"Does that shock you?" Maria asked.

"Oh, not at all," Misty responded. "It's just rare to have someone recognize that a good brain doesn't require a penis."

Maria smiled. I giggled. And Gibson almost fell off his horse.

"Good thing Crash didn't see you do that," I told Hoot.

"Your lady friend is full of surprises," Gibson chuckled.

"I'm counting on it."

We continued on into about a hundred acres of pastureland. I counted close to forty steers, a half dozen cows and one rather arrogant bull. The dusty white breed looked very much like American Brahman with a bit more of a Charles Laughton-style hunchback added.

"We raise enough beef for all of our employees and a little to send to market," Maria said. "As you can see, our herd is protected from jungle cats with the wall."

"That's a mighty tall wall just to keep cats out," Gibson said.

"The jungle has many aggressive predators. Some are pretty big. Our cattle, and us as well, are very enticing to meat eaters."

"The wall protects everything in the compound," Esteban

added.

From what I could see, the wall encircled at least two hundred acres of the property.

"That barrier had to be an expensive construction project," I said.

"And it's worth every cent," Maria explained. "Right after it was built, we had two incursions. One made it over the wall and another was able to tunnel under. Since then we've cleared a buffer zone on the other side. And now our vaqueros patrol both sides."

We rode up to a large wooden gate built into the stone barrier.

"Our scientific wonder is on the other side of the wall," Maria said, as she and Esteban dismounted and tossed their reins around a hitching post. "Our crops don't need protection from meat eaters."

Misty, Hoot and I stepped down and tethered our mounts. Esteban pulled up a large metal latch and then opened the gate about a foot. He quickly peeked through the opening, before swinging the gate wide enough for the rest of us. As soon as we walked through, Esteban closed the gate while using a stick to keep the latch open. Hoot and I looked in every direction for maniacal jungle cats that could have been waiting for a two-gringo cowboy lunch.

Instead, we faced a cornfield that made Iowa corn look like Bermuda grass.

"Scientific wonder!" a smiling Misty exclaimed.

Every towering stalk held at least two or three Louisville Slugger-sized ears of corn.

"Wow!" Gibson said. "Last time I grew corn in my garden, I was lucky to get one jackrabbit-sized ear per stalk."

"This is the fruition of Dr. LaFond's efforts," Maria boasted with a smile. "Do you see how this can be a game changer, not only in your efforts to supply food to troops and allies, but in defeating world hunger?"

"So are you looking to sell corn, seed or what?" I asked.

"Or what," Maria answered. "We can supply you with the chemicals, fertilizer if you want to call it that, so your country can produce the crops you need."

"This is not a hybrid plant?"

"No. This is just a field of sweet corn, enhanced with our G-719 product washed into the soil. Right after we plant, we treat the soil and then irrigate once. That's all it takes. In drier climates, you will have to continue to irrigate, but one treatment of G-719 will do the trick."

"Does your product work on other crops?" Misty asked.

"It works best on corn. Cotton also gets a little boost. It doesn't affect beans in any way. Many other vegetables, unfortunately, curl up and die. So we are still experimenting."

"What's in the product?" I asked.

"I'll let Dr. LaFond respond to that," Maria said. "As soon as you are through looking around here, we'll ride back to her lab."

I stood there with my head tilted back, looking up at the amazing maize and thought, "This must be what Alice felt like when she entered Wonderland." I reached up to pull down an ear so I could taste the giant corn. Then things got a little "curiouser."

I started to peel off the husk, and jumped back falling on my behind as a corn earworm the size of a dachshund twisted its head to face me. "Holy shit!"

Misty and Hoot looked accusingly at Maria.

"As I was about to explain," she said, "we haven't worked all the bugs out of the product yet."

"Good thing you didn't taste that," Gibson stated. "I wouldn't want to have to start calling you Curly Bunyon."

"The corn doesn't have that affect on people," Maria said defensively.

"How do you know?" Misty asked.

At that moment, Esteban gasped. He had walked several yards away along the edge of the field. I ran up to see what he was staring at, then stopped dead as I looked at an area of crushed stalks with a hoof sticking out. Silently, we entered the field and found the stalks were crushed in a circular formation that looked like it had been swatted by a giant tennis racket.

In the center of the circle was a steer's head. To the side I found another hoof attached to leg bones.

"What the hell did this?" I said.

"Something had to have gone over the fence and brought the steer back with it," Misty surmised. "And I'd bet acorns against alligators it wasn't big corn worms."

"Well if it were jungle cats, they had to have held a dance after their feast to have created this crop formation," Gibson said.

"Calm down everyone," Maria pleaded. "The steer could have been rustled by Indians. Members of the Amahuaca tribe roam this area along the Amazon."

"You're sayin' jungle natives were able to scale your wall, grab a steer and drag him back out here for dinner?" Gibson asked.

Esteban seemed extremely agitated. He kept repeating, "Lenda!"

Maria shouted at him in Portuguese.

"What's that all about?" I asked. "Who's Linda?"

"Lenda," she repeated. "Legend. The vaqueros tell stories about a jungle beast that haunts the river. Legend is described as a gigantic ten-foot-long creature that looks like a black scorpion with the head of a jaguar."

The bug-eyed foreman nodded his head up and down while tightly gripping his rifle.

"It's just superstition," she said. "This was only an Indian raiding party. Nothing more."

"I think we should look around a bit more," I said to Gibson. "But first, let's get Misty and Maria back inside the walls."

The two ladies walked back to the wooden door. Esteban started to follow them, until I placed a hand on his shoulder. "Hold on, pard," I said. "The three of us are armed. We can protect ourselves. When we get the ladies back to safety, we need to return and see if we can find any clues as to who or what did this."

I thought the foreman was going to be sick.

As we mounted our horses, Maria said, "You really don't have to return. There will be nothing out of the ordinary to find. Unlike the Indians in your country, our natives are still pretty wild. They hunt with poison arrows and darts. Some tribes still shrink heads."

Her assurances didn't seem to be helping Esteban's disposition.

"And now and then, they will rustle a head or two of cattle."

"I still want to look around," I said. "But first, I have a few things I would like to ask Dr. LaFond."

As we rode back toward the lab, a passel of questions swirled in my head. "What could have taken that steer over the wall?

How were the cornstalks flattened? What's with the giant corn worms? Do Brazilian Indians eat their meat without cooking it? Would Misty enjoy going to Barney's Beanery with me?"

The laboratory was made of a combination of stone and heavy hardwood beams. Attached to the building, the greenhouse was as large as a skating rink. We rode up to the front entrance and tethered our aristocratic-looking horses to a hitching post.

"I told Dr. LaFond to expect us," Maria said, while holding the front door open.

We entered a very welcoming room filled with comfortable furniture and decorated with a mixture of Spanish and western art. I recognized a couple of amazing Frederic Remington paintings on the wall.

"Not exactly what I'd expect to see in a laboratory," I said.

"Anita's late father was from Arizona," Maria said. "The doctor grew up with her mother in Argentina. This room reflects her mixed heritage."

An ornate, wrought iron, circular stairway filled one corner of the room. I assumed there would be bedrooms upstairs. A modern, yellow, swinging door looked out of place next to a wall-mounted southwestern tapestry. We heard laughing coming from the room behind the door.

"I believe she is in the kitchen. Let's take a look." Maria opened the swinging door into a very modern kitchen.

"Hello," said a lovely auburn-haired woman wearing a flowery housedress partially covered by an apron. "Welcome. My friend and I were just having a delightful conversation."

"Hi ya, Curly, Hoot," Nick chuckled. "Hello again, Misty. You haven't tired of the flack yet I see."

"This is Dr. Anita LaFond," Maria introduced us. "Anita, these Americans have a couple of questions regarding our research."

"Wonderful. I do so love to talk about our work. But, please, sit down and have a cup of coffee," the slender scientist motioned toward a large craftsman-style table with unique wooden chairs that clashed with the modern appliances. She was one of those naturally lovely women who never seem to need makeup. I could understand why Nick was obviously attracted to her.

We pulled up chairs and relaxed while the doctor poured steaming mugs of java. Esteban stood stoically near the door.

Nick brought over a half-empty casserole dish. "Curly! You've got to have a piece of Anita's amazing cornbread. It's to die for!"

My jaw dropped as Hoot, Misty and I turned and, silently, gaped at Nick.

"What's wrong? Do I have crumbs on my chin?"

"As I told you," Maria said. "The corn has no adverse affects on people."

The doctor began to laugh. "They must have discovered a corn worm."

"Yes," Maria answered. "And even the worms don't have a problem with the corn. We've found that when we treat the soil and then irrigate, some insects have a negative reaction to G-719. But we are working on that, aren't we Anita."

"Oh, yes. Our latest growth system, G-719, is extremely safe. And, I believe the world will soon become a much happier place because of this scientific breakthrough. After you have your coffee, I will show you some of our wonders in the greenhouse."

Nick sat quietly with question marks in his eyes, while Hoot and I continued to watch him out of the corners of ours.

"Thank you for the coffee," Misty said. "But I would really like to get a look in your greenhouse."

"Certainly," the doctor replied. "Follow me."

We left the kitchen and walked into a short hallway that led to metal double doors.

"So what's the problem," Nick whispered while we walked.

"Oh, nothing really," I answered in my best inside voice. "Just keep calm and don't eat any more cornbread."

From the look of him, that didn't answer his question.

"Oh, my!" Misty exclaimed, as we entered the greenhouse, which was a good thirty degrees warmer and quite humid.

"It is a shock to newcomers," the doctor said. "Once you get used to it, you will hardly notice the difference in temperature."

We faced row after row of boxed plants. Some were jungle ferns, while many others were crops of various sizes. While looking upward at a grapevine that twisted up to the glass ceiling, I felt something brush against my boot.

"Holy cats!" Gibson exclaimed.

There were many small cats running around the floor and climbing up the boxes. All of them were wearing thin blue collars.

"Don't worry about my babies," the doctor said. "They have free run of the place. They're not only delightful company, but they keep the mice from getting out of hand."

"Oh, I just love kittens," Misty announced, while picking one up and caressing it.

"I have a kitten at home," I said.

"You're not talkin' about that rotten Spade, are you?" Hoot spat.

I growled at the mean man.

"And he has his name on his collar," the blonde fed said. She then thrust him toward my face. "Curly, meet little Denny."

With a fake grin, I nuzzled the little dust ball against my cheek, while holding back a sneeze.

"I know you research scientists sometimes use lab animals," a concerned Misty said. "But you don't experiment on kittens, do you?"

"Never!" LaFond said. "These kitties are my friends. And I would never hurt my friends."

"Wow!" Nick exclaimed. "Look at this!"

He stood in a row of cornstalks rising out of boxes to almost reach the glass ceiling.

"Corn has been our biggest success," the auburn-haired doctor said. "But we believe we can do better."

I motioned toward an area of about twenty feet of twisted cotton plants.

"Cotton has had mixed results," she explained. "The plants have increased in size while the bolls are small and somewhat useless."

She pulled a boll husk off to show a twisted chunk of fiber with black and yellow growths in it.

"I'm currently experimenting with different formulae for various crops, including cotton, rice, grapes, berries and melons. But for right now, our G-719 is ready to be exported for use with corn."

"So some crops react to the formula like it was a herbicide?" I asked.

"Yes. Growers must be very careful not to use our formula near other crops. That's why I recommend the system only be sold to commercial farmers who produce corn."

"What about jungle plants? Has there been any reaction there from your product?"

"As you have seen, jungle foliage is already tall and dense. There would be no reason to mess around with that growth. And our experimental crops are all on cleared land separate from the forest."

As I made my way through the foliage and felines, I noticed an area of about 500 square feet that was boarded up in a corner. There was a padlock on the wood door. "What's in there?"

"That's a storage area for chemicals," LaFond said. "I have to keep everything locked up and separate so as not to contaminate any of my experiments."

We walked down several rows of normal garden plants as well as an area of orchids.

"Those are there for my own enjoyment," LaFond said. "Natural orchids are beautiful and I don't see any reason to mess with that."

"What about these?" Gibson asked, while standing in front of an approximately twenty-foot row of strange plants.

"Those are all carnivorous," she said. "The Amazon has an enormous variety of meat-eating plants. Aren't they amazing?"

"Weird," Hoot said. "But I'll bet they keep the flies down."

"Yes, they have many reasons to exist in the environment," Anita answered.

"I've seen enough for now," Misty said, while turning toward the door. "I should discuss this with my team."

She caressed Denny, kissed him on the top of his head and put him down. We exited the greenhouse and welcomed the slight chill we felt as we walked back to the comfortable room with the beautiful Remington paintings. While Maria and Anita discussed something near the kitchen door, I pulled Hoot, Nick and Misty aside.

"Nick, I want you to stay with Misty while Hoot, Esteban and I ride back to the cornfield."

Nick wiggled his eyebrows and looked at Misty. "Hey, no problem, pal. We could have a couple of cold beers."

"Misty will fill you in on where we are going and why." I added, "I hope you enjoyed the cornbread."

Gibson reached over, put his hand on Nick's head and then slid it toward himself, as if he were measuring to see if the chauffeur had grown taller. Misty chuckled.

"We're gonna look around and then come right back," I said. "If we're not back by sundown, round up Buck, Crash, Donovan and anybody else you can trust and come and get us. Misty will draw you a map to the gate."

"Hell, Curly," the blonde beauty said. "If you're not back by sunset, I'll lead them through the gate!"

I thanked the doctor for her hospitality and we left. As I went out the door, Misty grabbed me by my arm, pulling me to a halt. I looked into her large blue eyes and smiled. Without saying a word, she leaned in and kissed me on the lips. I'm not sure what happened next, except the temperature suddenly felt like I had returned to the greenhouse.

Misty and Maria walked their horses back toward the stables with Nick tagging along. I realized I was standing quite still, alone on the porch. Stumbling to the hitching post with a glazed expression, I heard Gibson say, "You still comin', Curly?"

I straightened my face, pulled my Stetson firmly onto my head, climbed back on my horse and rode off into the pastureland with Hoot and Esteban.

****

The steers were calm, unaware that one of their brothers had been rustled and devoured. It's as if it didn't matter in life's plan. I guess cattle are all like that since sooner or later they all end up on a menu.

When we arrived at the gate, Esteban held it open while we exited the walled property. I dismounted and positioned a six-inch-diameter branch to hold the door open. I certainly didn't want the latch to drop on the inside and leave us locked out. We tethered our horses to a shrub near the wall and advanced on foot.

I led the way along the tremendously tall cornfield until we reached the crushed stalks. Walking into the formation, I noticed two things. One, the dead steer's remains were no longer in the crop circle. And, two, there were more circles butting up against the first one.

"What the hell is crushing these cornstalks?" Gibson asked.

"And how are they doing it in such a short time?"

I had no idea. To cover such a large area, one would have had to use a big, heavy tractor. But how did they make the areas into perfect circles? And where did the steer head go?

"Let's just see what we can discover," I said. "Hoot, take this first circle and see if you can find anything that could tell us how it was created. Esteban and I will check out the next couple of areas."

The ranch foreman and I crossed into the next formation of crushed stalks and found there were two path-like swaths about the width of an Army tank that entered the other side. And yet, there were no tracks that would have identified the culprits as motorized heavy equipment.

Esteban looked like he was being led to the gallows.

"Stop, senhor," he pleaded. "Morte aguarda!"

"Huh?"

"Death awaits! A lenda, legend has returned!"

"What are you talkin' about?"

"Rancho Grandé exports death! We must go back! And you must leave the Amazon!"

Esteban's frantic behavior increased as he waved his arms and babbled.

"Easy does it, Esteban," I urged. "Let's just calm down and maybe you could explain what you're worried about."

At that moment he stepped back and screamed. Orange sludge boiled up around his feet.

"What the hell?" I ran forward and looked where he had been standing. A large, crushed corn worm thrashed from under the stalks, emitting a whispered roar through the thick, bilious liquid flowing out of its mouth.

The panic-stricken foreman's eyes bugged out, as he leaped back to his feet, screamed and ran into the standing cornfield.

"Esteban!" I yelled.

I could hear him crushing through the stalks for a moment, then silence.

"What's goin' on over there?" the Hooter hollered from the other crop circle.

"I'm not sure. Esteban stepped on a corn worm and then ran off." I had barely finished my answer when we heard the shot.

"That's from his Springfield," I said, as four more shots were fired.

Then, a loud scream that Fay Wray would have envied hit our ears.

"Shit!" I exclaimed, as I yanked my Luger from my pocket and ran into the cornfield toward where the sound appeared to originate. The stalks slapped my face and did their best to trip me as I thrashed my way forward.

I didn't have a clue as to what the heck was going on. All I knew was that Esteban had obviously lost his mind. I just hoped he wouldn't shoot me, while thinking I was some legendary creature of his imagination.

"I found him!" Gibson yelled from approximately twenty yards to my right.

I shoved my way through the incredibly tall cornstalks toward his voice. Everything about that morning had been strange but, at that instant, reality took a hard left turn into a bizarre environment littered with unimaginable deadly creatures.

I stepped onto a swath of smashed stalks about the size of a firebreak. Gibson stood not far away, waving his arms to get my attention. I started to run toward him, but slowed down as my eyes focused on what was crumpled on the path near his feet. The bottom half of a man was sticking up out of the ground, sliced apart at his gun belt, with what was left of his intestines strewn across the crushed cornstalks.

"What the hell, Hoot? Is that our man?"

"Yep. The blood trail leads toward the jungle," the cowboy said. "Whatever knocked down these crops dragged the rest of him thataway."

With our pistols held in our right hands, we began following the long smear of blood laced with small chunks of meat. The light of day abandoned us as we passed through a wall of greenery into the thick, damp rainforest jungle. Branches were broken and rocks pushed aside by what we were beginning to expect might be a real nightmare. There were weird prints punched into the mud along the path that certainly gave me the willies.

A little bit earlier, we had been told a story about a ten-foot-long, black, scaly scorpion with the head of a jaguar that hunted cattle and men. At the time, I chuckled at what I considered a typical campfire horror tale to frighten children enough to keep them out of the jungle. But the farther we traveled into the rainforest, the more I began to wonder.

An ungodly scream set both of us back onto our butts as a very large reddish howler monkey swung down out of the jungle canopy, dropped to the ground next to us and ran toward where we had entered the tangled green ferns, vines and trees.

"Holy crap, Curly! Something really scared that guy!"

"Probably just a coincidence. Howler monkeys all sound like that."

Another scream turned into a roar, just as a large spotted jungle cat raced out of the foliage, leaped over both of us and followed the noisy primate.

"Then again, something may have scared them both."

We jumped to our feet, holding our guns in front of us as we advanced. I watched to the right while Hoot scanned to the left.

"Curly," Gibson said quietly. "You remember that giant scorpion we heard about."

"Yeah."

"I found it."

"Oh, shit!"

"It's dead!"

"Wonderful," I said. "Finally a lucky break."

"Not exactly," he said, looking upward into the thick growth.

I walked over to him and leaned my head back to see what he meant. Nearly fifty feet in the air above us, a ten-foot black scorpion carcass was tangled in a mammoth web, dwarfed by the huge, furry, venomous banana spider that was sucking the fluids from its body. One of the dead creature's claws, broken from its twisted remains, dropped through the branches and crashed to the ground next to us. Then the sucking sound ended as the spider lifted its head and turned eight piercing black eyes down toward us. The red fur of its mouth dripped as the feasting arachnid began an evil clicking sound.

Hoot was first to break free from the beast's hypnotic stare. Then we both raced back toward the corn, doing our best to catch up with and pass the jungle cat and howling monkey, in our attempts to escape with our lives.

CHAPTER 6. CHASING THE DRAGON

Branches, thorns and sharp leaves nicked my face and hands as I fought my way through the thick jungle foliage. Hearing shots being fired behind me, I stopped and turned to see Gibson facing the other way with his pistol held in front of him, smoke lifting from its barrel.

"I got it!" he hollered.

The gigantic spider was about thirty feet behind us, standing on its back four legs clawing the air while making that clicking sound. Purple fluid poured out of a socket where one of its eyes belonged. Hoot fired another shot as I joined him in blasting away at the creature. The beast's ugly face was peppered with oozing bullet holes as it teetered to the side and crumpled onto the rainforest's mulch-covered floor – legs thrashing as life slowly deserted the venomous monster.

"Thank God spiders don't have shells like scorpions," I said.

"Yeah," Hoot said, while holstering his pistol. "Esteban's .30-06 slugs must have just bounced off that critter's carcass."

"And yet the spider was able to catch and kill the scorpion."

"Nature's mysterious plan."

"Especially in these woods."

Another roar came from somewhere in the distance, as if the living jungle was aware of the monster's death.

"We better get the hell out of here," I said to empty space. Hoot had already started running.

Daylight slammed into our eyes as we exited the rainforest and reentered the "scientific wonder" turned "freakish" cornfield. Hoot stopped, wiped sweat from his forehead and looked at me with concern in his eyes.

"I need to catch my breath," he said.

"Good shootin' back there."

63

"I just hope we don't have to shoot a fifteen-foot-tall, eight-legged Nick Danby when we get back."

"Dr. LaFond said the corn is safe."

"And you trust her?"

"Not now," I said. "But think about it. Spiders and scorpions don't eat corn. They eat meat. Yet, like the corn seed, they have to have been somehow infected by her G-719 formula."

I scratched my head and thought about the squashed earworm.

"All of the freak insects we've seen so far have one thing in common. They crawl around in the soil. So, just like the corn seeds, they were doused in her chemical fertilizer and then irrigated."

I looked down at my feet and cringed. "We better just get on out of here. Who knows what else may have been crawling around during their planting efforts?"

We started on our way back to the gate when a crunching sound caused the hair on my neck to straighten out like porcupine quills. We froze in our tracks. Something close by was stomping around like Babe the big blue ox from folklore.

Both of us assumed the prone position and low crawled, infantry style, through the corn toward the sound. The stalks thinned and I threw my right hand up to silently let Hoot know to halt. With eyes bugged, we both gaped toward an area that was becoming a crop circle.

With a terrified expression on its dead face, our friend the howler monkey was broken and twisted in the center of the newly stomped stalks. An at-least-ten-foot, scale-covered scorpion faced its poisoned simian lunch while walking sideways around it, creating a perfect circle. A steamroller couldn't have done a better job of leveling the area, as did that heavy, scaly nightmare. The vision was as amazing as it was terrifying – a monstrous dance of death.

Gibson reached over and pulled on my shirt. I silently turned my head to shush him when I felt the tremor. The ground beneath us rumbled and then started to lift. I rolled back as dirt clods tumbled across me. Gibson was almost buried in the moving, lifting soil.

A chattering sound filled the air and something soft pushed against me. I peeked up to the top of the crumbling berm and, quickly, pushed backward away from my position. The large squishy leg that had bumped into me was replaced by another, then another and another. Crawling out of the freshly created, truck-size hole in front of us was a centipede that, if it were a balloon, looked like it could have floated over a complete block during Macy's Thanksgiving Day Parade. (Maybe my estimation was a tad exaggerated. It may not have been a complete block long, but certainly long enough to devour the Mickey and Pluto balloons.)

The scorpion rocked back on its tail, snapping its massive claws at the huge multi-legged venomous myriapod. The two deadly goliaths faced each other in a battle to the death, with the late howler monkey allegedly scheduled for dessert. The scorpion lifted its tail to the left of its head and scurried forward to attack its rival. The centipede, which had the room to advertise the Atchison, Topeka and Santa Fe on its carcass, seemed to expect the assault. It recoiled like a rattler and feigned a roll to its right, only to twist its segmented body and drop down snapping its jaws around its enemy's weapon. With greasy orange fluid flying into the air, the centipede ripped the scorpion's tail from its body; then wrapped itself around its prey, gripping with more legs than a chorus line of the Radio City Music Hall Rockettes.

"Quickly!" I exclaimed, as Hoot and I pushed the dirt off of us and started running.

We could hear howling, smashing and slurping as the centipede finalized its victory. We ran for a good fifteen minutes before slowing to a stop so we could gasp for air. I looked around and saw we were still in the cornfield.

"Where the hell are we?" Hoot asked.

"I'm not really sure," I answered. "Although I think we're a bit farther away from the gate."

"Wonderful!"

Our nerves were already on edge when we heard the rumbling.

"Oh, crap!" Gibson exclaimed. "Here comes another big bug!"

I listened a moment. "Hang on, there, Hoot. That sounds familiar."

Cautiously, I moved toward the sound. The stalks thinned and I could see a dirt road. Then we both saw the Ford tractor moving in our direction. Hoot smiled and started to step out of the corn to wave down the driver. I grabbed him and pulled him back.

"What the...?"

"Let's just wait a moment," I explained. "We don't know who that is or where he's goin'."

"It's got to be a Rancho Grandé hand. We're obviously still on that property."

"Yeah, but take a good look at that driver."

We stayed back in the stalks and watched as the tractor went by.

"He doesn't look like one of Esteban's vaqueros," I said. "In fact, the driver looks more like an extra on an old Rudolph Valentino flicker."

The tanned, bearded farm worker was wearing what looked like a dirty sheet with sleeves. He had a gray wool shawl wrapped around his neck and flowing off his right shoulder. On his head was a brown piece of cloth wrapped and knotted like something Tom Tyler's slaves might have worn in the new Universal horror flick, "The Mummy's Hand." A leather belt around his waist held the sheet in place while supporting an ornate curved knife.

"He's some kind of Arab," Gibson said.

"Yeah, and take a look at the rifle he has attached to the tractor."

"Holy crap. It's a Mauser Gewehr."

The Gewehr 98 bolt-action rifle, made by Mauser, was the standard weapon of the Kaiser's infantry in The Great War. I wondered what an Arab was doing in Brazil while armed with a German rifle.

"I think we now have enough questions to support following that guy," I said. "We'll stay to the side of the road so we can jump into the bushes if we need to."

"He's already out of sight."

"True. But Ford tractor tires do leave pretty clear trails on dirt roads for, oh, say, a well-known western pathfinder of the silver screen to track. Do you happen to know where we could find one of those guys?"

The big grump frowned and started our new hike. With our eyes wide open, we made our way along the side of the road. After a while, the cornfields vanished and were replaced by tilled dirt and shrubs.

"It's been a while since breakfast," Gibson said. "I could eat a giant corn worm."

"Really?"

"No! But I'm hungry."

I was too. But I also knew we had left the gated compound to find answers to some questions. And after a couple of hours of investigation, we had garnered very few answers and a hell of a lot more new questions.

I figured the tractor would lead us to some, hopefully, innocent human activity. If we came upon a crew of friendly farmworkers, we could probably get something to eat and maybe a ride back to the gate. If "innocent" didn't turn out to be the operative word, I supposed us two old war vets could commandeer a tractor for our return trip.

****

Following another hour of stumbling along the dirt road, we stopped, dropped and rolled into heavy grass. There was a large stone-built warehouse approximately fifty yards in front of us. Parked next to it were the aforementioned tractor and three trucks that looked like they were built for beer delivery following the demise of Prohibition.

"I'd like to take a look in that building," Gibson said.

"I'm a little more interested in that field on the other side," I added.

Bright pink flowers covered a very large acreage of land on the other side of the stone building.

"So they grow pretty flowers," Gibson said. "At least there aren't any corn worms involved."

"Let's move over behind that truck so we can get a better look," I said, as we scurried as quickly and quietly as we could toward the building.

We knelt down next to a Ford delivery truck.

"Now that worries me," I said. "Those flowers are poppies."

"Kinda tall, ain't they?"

"Yep."

The pretty pink flowers covered the top of the plants at about seven feet in the air. The seedpods had to be at least six inches in diameter.

"A giant corn worm could have a high old time in those king-size opium poppies," Hoot remarked.

"Now we know Dr. LaFond's G-719 formula has been successful on more than just corn and bugs," I thought out loud. "If a few fields like this one are planted in Persia, or whatever they call it now, Turkey, China and/or South and Central America, the civilized world could be destroyed by a biblical-sized flood of heroin."

We held very still as a parade of uniquely attired men filed out of the warehouse. The Arab tractor driver with his German rifle in his right hand led the group, followed by six thin, reddish-skinned, almost naked men who had to be Amazonian natives. They wore loincloths and carried bowls containing wide, curved scraping knives. All of the Brazilian Indians had Moe Howard-style haircuts and ropes tied between their ankles, hobbling them from being able to run. The final parade participant was another Arab carrying four wooden flat trays, two under each arm. A holstered Luger hung from his leather belt.

I started to say something to Hoot, but halted myself as two more work crews filed out of the warehouse and trekked toward the poppy field. Once they had entered their destination, we walked around the back of the structure to an open door. I didn't see any more workers inside, so we silently entered the facility and moved around behind a pile of cloth bags.

There was an approximately hundred-square-foot area of the flat trays sitting on concrete blocks. Each of the trays contained a couple of inches of brown gunk, obviously drying opium. Next to that, was a stack of wooden boxes, many with their lids off showing they were not quite completely filled with cloth-covered rolls of the brown tar.

It looked like the operation probably shipped out raw opium to be refined into heroin at other facilities. The massive amount of product that we could see just waiting to be shipped was far larger than anything I had ever heard or read about.

Having been a crime-beat newspaper reporter at the *Los Angeles Examiner* prior to becoming a studio flack, I had covered a lot of deadly situations that could be traced directly to illegal drugs that were being shipped into America to feed the need of a variety of addicted losers – some of whom worked in the entertainment industry.

Gibson tapped me on the shoulder. When I turned, I saw him pointing toward one of the bags we were hiding behind. "G-719" was stamped on the cloth.

"Now we know how Dom Sebastian and sister Maria were able to pay for their opulent compound and wall," Hoot whispered. "We should get back and report to Donovan. Big Jim needs to know about this place."

"Yeah. I don't think our State Department procurement specialists need to work any deals with anyone brought to this ranch by the Sebastians."

We hunkered down at the sound of a door opening from a sectioned off area of the warehouse. Located at the far end, it looked like it might have been a meeting room or office space. Three more dusty Arabs backed out the door as someone lectured them in their own language from within. They turned and ran out of the warehouse. Within seconds, we heard all three of the big trucks start up and drive away.

"I think we're down to just one honcho in headquarters," I whispered. "Let's see what he has to say."

With our pistols in our right hands, we quietly advanced to the office door. I could see our adversary, standing facing away from us, wearing a long, clean, white robe, black riding boots, a black belt supporting a flashy curved knife in a scabbard, and a square of checkered material that looked like a small tablecloth from an Italian restaurant held on his head by two twisted cords.

I cleared my throat and the man turned to face us. He had thick white hair with a pencil-thin mustache to match.

"Well, hello there, Dom Sebastian," I said. "No wonder you don't have time to socialize."

His surprised expression quickly morphed into the most evil smile I had ever seen.

His surprised expression quickly morphed into the most evil smile I had ever seen.

"My, my," he purred through sharp, white teeth. "You're both obviously smarter than you look."

Hoot reached over and relieved the asshole of his big curved knife.

"And you don't look much like a Brazilian aristocrat any more," I said. "Perhaps you might enlighten us on a few questions we have concerning this operation of yours."

"Please, sit down. What would you two armed infidels like to know?"

"Do you have anything to eat in here?" Gibson asked.

"I am sorry. I seem to be deficient in my hosting duties. There's a big tray of cornbread on the table. Please help yourselves."

"Never mind," Hoot said. "I'm not that hungry."

"So, improving corn crops to fight world hunger isn't really your focus?" I said.

"What was your first clue?" the smarmy scoundrel said.

"Spill it, asshole!" Gibson cut to the chase. "Why the summit? Why play botanic humanitarian? What are you gonna do with all this devil's crop?"

"Excellent! Now that's more like the American cowboy we all love to hate. That devil's crop is going to make me one of the richest men in the world. It will also lower the prices many of your Hollywood pals are paying to chase the dragon. In fact, I spent a few years in that crazy town during the silent-movie days supplying some of your big-time silver screen junkies, many of whom are no longer with us."

"The summit…" I reminded.

"I was hoping to get a big pile of Roosevelt's American dollars to ship our growth product to your farmers."

"Why would you want to help American farmers?"

"Au contraire, mon amie. Your countrymen will be delighted to see what our product does for their crops," he said, "until they see what it also does to the insects in the ground. Wouldn't it be wonderful to go into a theatre and see a Pathé Newsreel showing a gigantic potato bug smashing cars and eating school children in Idaho, or possibly a ten-foot vinegaroon dining on divorcees in Reno?"

"So the whole corn miracle is an attempt to sabotage both our environment and economy."

"You are a winner. Give the man $64," the facetious fanatic quipped. "We developed G-719 specifically for our opium crop. When we discovered the entomological side effects, we knew we had more bangs for that buck."

Realizing our interrogation was taking a while, I sent Hoot to watch at the door to the warehouse. I didn't want any enemy towel hats sneaking up on us.

"So Maria is not your sister?"

"No, she's not. I picked her up from a chorus line in Rio de Janeiro. She's turned into a pretty good actress."

"Where did the funding come from that created this operation?"

"I have backers from a variety of countries who, like us, would like to see all decadent Americans wallowing in a giant gutter of drugs and bugs. Not all of my backers get along with each other, but we all have a few enemies in common. The Soviet Socialists hate Christians and Capitalists while Hitler's National Socialists hate Jews. And, of course, we hate them all. In fact, there are many Moslems who just aren't quite kosher either, to my tastes anyway. We hate them as well."

Sebastian, or whatever his real name was, certainly had to be insane. I figured I had better get a wiggle on and get out of that joint before my luck ran out. I knew I could always question the chatty Arab in safer confines.

"Stand up, sheik shithead! We gotta get back to your ranch to stop this operation in its tracks!"

"Oh, you're too late for that, Curly. Those trucks that just left were carrying full loads of G-719 to be flown to your beloved Midwest breadbasket."

"But there hasn't been any contracts negotiated for that poison!"

"We gave up on negotiations this morning when you started your Nancy Drew-like investigation. The growth fertilizer is being sent as our little gift to your farmers. We are also shipping G-719 to several opium producing cartels in this hemisphere as well as my home country."

"Hurry up, Curly!" Hoot called from the warehouse. "We're about to have company."

"Let's go, asshole!" I yelled.

"I'm not going anywhere," the evil man formerly known as Dom Sebastian said. "You've already lost and I've won!"

I saw the grenade pin flick away from his hand and, instantly, I ran out of the room, slammed the door behind me and dived over a pile of fertilizer bags. The explosion disintegrated the door, shredded the inside of the office and left my ears ringing like a Frisco trolley without brakes. I looked at the other side of the bags I had used for protection and found they were littered with shrapnel, splinters and one or two pieces of greasy red bone.

Gibson was firing his pistol and hollering, "What the hell did you do?"

"It must have been something I said. We gotta get back to the main house, pronto!"

The three Indian work teams were seated in the dirt with one of the armed Arabs standing over them. The other five Arabs were spread out and advancing toward the warehouse.

"Our two pistols aren't that capable against those German rifles," Gibson said, as a bullet ripped a chunk out of the doorframe near his ear.

He was right. And time was running out. We needed to neutralize the attacking Arabs and get back to the ranch in time to stop any flights containing G-719.

"Keep firing," I said, while tossing him my Luger.

I frantically searched the warehouse for anything that could turn the odds back in our favor. The grenade explosion had knocked down a stack of wooden boxes in front of the dead fanatic's former office. I grabbed a metal bar and started prying the tops off of them. The first three contained small, folded, colorful rugs. "Damn!" I kept prying. "Pay dirt!" One held a single grenade in its own canister.

I ran to the door with the grenade and told the Hooter, "Use this to slow 'em down. I'll see what else I can find."

The cowboy gripped the hand-held bomb, pulled the pin and tossed it toward the closest enemy. "Special delivery!"

The Arab's eyes bugged out further than a corn worm's just before the pineapple exploded, shredding a good part of the front of him and tearing it through and out the back of him. The other four riflemen backed away to find cover while the Arab who was guarding the Indians left his post to join his fellow troopers.

"Aha!" I hollered as I yanked the lid off a box, finding the most beautiful apparatus ever invented. I picked up the new black .45 caliber Thomson submachine gun, slapped on the hundred-round drum magazine, jacked a round into the chamber, rushed to the open door and, with a smile that said "Life is beautiful," pulled the trigger. Feeling like Jimmy Cagney against prohibitionists, I ripped the ground up to the Arab on the left and kept shredding across him and his buddies all the way to the last one on the right.

When the smoke cleared, Hoot and I inspected the damage. Only one of the Arabs was still breathing, and that seemed to be just a mild gurgling through three holes in his chest. I looked down as the red and white froth stopped bubbling and he joined his fellow travelers on their trip to whatever reward they had believed they might receive.

With my pocketknife, I cut the ropes that hobbled the Indian slaves. They were quite grateful and, although we didn't understand each other's language, it seemed like they wanted to help. I thought a moment. Then I pulled a box of wooden matches out of my pocket. Taking a piece of a dry shrub, I set it on fire and then touched off an area of the poppies. I handed the matches to one of the newly freed men and all of them began to nod their heads and smile.

Then Hoot and I ran to the tractor. I climbed in the driver's seat while Gibson stood behind me. I pushed the starter and the engine rumbled like it was brand new.

"Floor it!" Hoot said.

"Just hang on to that Thompson, pal," I said, while checking my Tom Mix radio premium compass. "I'll get us there."

As we started down the dirt road, the burning poppy fields were beginning to send up dark oily smoke while the warehouse was almost fully engulfed in flame.

"It's getting late, Curly. It'll be sundown pretty soon."

"Time flies when you're havin' fun."

I pushed the Ford tractor to its maximum speed, which was still slow enough that two corn worms and a congressman on his way to the confessional could have passed us. I scanned to the front of us while the Hooter kept his eyes peeled for big bugs and Arabs.

My mind was spinning with questions and fears. I was worried about Misty. She was still back at the ranch, but so was Maria, who was part of the conspiracy. Dr. LaFond also had to be as crazy as a bedbug, herself. She developed the poison that turned opium poppies, cornstalks and insects into monsters. "What else did she have up her sleeve?" I wondered.

And I really hoped I wouldn't find Nick climbing the mansion wall while trying to spin a web. Rick would fire me if I had to bring Nick back in a cage.

We were skirting the massive cornfields that, I was sure, still held a myriad of dangers stomping around on their scaly, hairy, pointy big feet while looking for tasty victims. The air started to chill as the sun dropped behind the tall rainforest trees and the sounds of night began to increase. I turned on the small headlights and, within moments, could see a part of the great wall in the distance. I sighed, knowing that soon I'd be able to hold Misty in my arms and protect her from the demons of Rancho Grandé.

The first shot ricocheted off the engine hood.

"Bedouins!" Gibson shouted.

"What?"

"Arabs!" he explained, pointing to the right.

I could see the cornstalks moving as something ran along just out of our sight. Then one of the robed rascals pushed aside a couple of the plants and fired his German rifle. Immediately Hoot sent enough .45 caliber slugs from the Thompson to practically cut the man in half. Then another Arab fired a shot and jacked his bolt to put a second round in the chamber, but just not quite fast enough. I took him out with my Luger while Gibson raked a line along the front of the cornstalks, leading to two more robed enemies dropping forward to join the dust in death, where their carcasses probably remained until some lucky hungry bug came along.

I yanked the steering wheel, making the tractor zigzag, as if that might help keep us from being shot. We continued to take fire, but the Arabs certainly weren't marksmen. I sighted my Luger on one crazy fool and pulled the trigger. I was out of ammo. Hoot saw the situation and blasted the man with the Thompson, pretty much removing the top of his head. Then I heard the misfire. The Thompson had jammed. Gibson drew his pistol, realizing at that moment he also lacked ammunition.

I slammed on the brakes, as a half dozen Arabs stepped directly in front of us. They obviously had heard the submachine gun jam and understood our situation. In a straight line across our path, the men smiled and pulled their large curved knives from their scabbards. One of them yelled some kind of an insult before spitting in our direction. Lifting their blades in the air, they all started screaming and running toward us.

I stood up on the tractor seat and prepared to leap into the middle of them, using my Luger as a club. Gibson jumped to the side of the Ford and put his fists up in his best John L. Sullivan pose. Oh, yeah. We were gonna die.

The attacking, screaming Arabs froze in their tracks and went silent. I saw their eyes roll down to inspect their bodies just before they fell on their faces.

"What the...?"

Gibson and I walked forward to where the robed enemy lay. Their faces, necks, hands and parts of their robes were covered with small darts. And they were dead.

Approximately twenty loincloth-wearing Amazon Indians walked out of the cornfield carrying blowguns. I recognized a few of the men we had freed earlier. One smiling familiar native held out the box of matches to return them to me. I smiled and mimed striking a match and then pointing at the cornfield. Once again, we had communicated.

I picked up two German rifles and stacked them next to the tractor seat. One of the late cloth-hat killers carried a holstered Luger. I was able to find three full magazines of which I shoved two in my pocket and the third in my pistol. Several of the Indians grinned while gathering the curved knives from their dart recipients.

By the time Gibson and I reached the wall, the natives had vanished and the cornfield was adding to an oily haze that promised a better morning. I smiled and slapped Hoot's back. "Well done, old friend. We've survived again."

The sound of horses got our attention. We looked up to see Buck, Crash, Donovan and Nick galloping along the wall toward us. The four men dismounted chuckling at our appearance.

"Hey, Hoot," Crash hollered. "Where'd you get the Warner Brothers violin?"

Gibson realized he was still holding the jammed Thompson. He tossed it to the ground and retrieved one of the German rifles from the tractor. I grabbed the other one.

"What are you guys trying to do with that cornfield?" Nick asked, over the sounds crackling out of the thirty-foot-high flames. "Make some Mount Rushmore-sized popcorn?"

"I thought you guys left on horses," Buck said.

"I thought you guys left on horses," Buck said.

"We did," I explained. "They should be tethered near the gate."

"Nope," Donovan said. "No horses and no gate either. But there are some pretty big splinters where the gate is supposed to be."

"Uh, oh," Gibson whispered.

"We gotta get back to the ranch," I said, "and the airfield! I'll explain on the way."

"Then you better mount up with us," Buck said, as he reached down to help me climb on behind him. "Our horses can make better time than your tractor."

"You can ride with me, Hoot," Nick offered.

"I'll ride up front," the rodeo champ responded, "as long as you promise not to sting me."

Nick looked confused, but slid back behind the saddle so Gibson could mount his horse in the front, with his rifle balanced in his lap behind the horn.

"Hey, Nick," I said. "Where's Misty?"

"Don't know. One minute she was waiting for me to bring back two beers and the next, she was gone."

All of us rode quickly back to the shattered gate while I did my best to explain the situation. Our four rescuers remained silent as I recounted our adventure. Hoot jumped in periodically to relay colorful descriptions, which may or may not have been exaggerated.

We rode up to where the large wooden gate had been. There were still shreds of wood hanging from hinges, and shattered boards littering the ground within a thirty-foot diameter. In the spot where we had tethered our horses, I found blood – lots of it.

"So some kind of giant bug ate your horses and trashed the gate?" Donovan asked.

"That's my guess," I said, as I climbed back up behind Buck.

"And that perpetrator could be a B-17-sized mutant spider, centipede, scorpion or corn worm?" Buck asked.

"More or less."

From the corner of my eye, I saw Nick's expression turn evil. Seated on his horse behind Gibson, the sneaky chauffeur reached into his pocket and removed a pencil. With the speed of a rattler, he tightly grabbed Hoot by the left shoulder, yelled "Sting!" and poked him in the back of his ear with the pencil.

Hoot's eyes bugged out as he yanked the reins, causing the horse to rear. Both men flew into the air and landed on their butts.

"You rat!" Gibson spat.

"Scorpion, actually," Nick said.

"Why did you do that?" Hoot yelled.

"I don't know why you're surprised," the facetious chauffeur said. "You knew I was Nick Danby when you let me ride in the back."

Donovan thought that was pretty funny, while Buck, once again, just rolled his eyes. At that moment I realized Nick was going to be just fine. But I wasn't that sure about Hoot.

CHAPTER 7. SAVAGE FLORA AND FAUNA

We rode through the opening in the fence and galloped toward the hacienda. Nick had to ride double with Crash.

"I've got to find Misty!" I hollered, when we reached the greenhouse. "Donovan, you and Crash should ride like the wind to the airfield. Stop any aircraft from leaving the area. Detain all pilots, crews and anyone scurrying around loading big bags and stuff. Especially, any Arabs."

"Those guys are obviously fanatical Moslems," Buck said. "You won't be able to detain them. You'll have to kill 'em."

"Buck," I said, "I'd like you and Hoot to head back to the hacienda. Round up the State Department crew. Keep an eye out for Misty. Get them all to a safe area. Don't trust anyone else. We'll join you just as soon as we search this place."

The G-man and the former Mesquiteer galloped away toward the airfield. Buck and Hoot took off for the hacienda, while Nick and I advanced cautiously into the stone lab building.

"That crazy Dr. LaFond may be in here," I said, while gripping my new rifle. "Keep your eyes open."

"It's hard to believe she could be evil," Nick whispered. "She seemed so sweet."

"Yeah, and you loved her cornbread."

The chauffeur wiped his mouth and spit. "Perhaps you're right."

The warm, comfortable front room with the Remington paintings wasn't quite as welcoming as it had been earlier. The silence sent my overactive neck hairs on edge, again. But there was something else I couldn't quite put my finger on.

I looked at the circular staircase in the corner. I hadn't thought much about it the last time we were there.

"Let's check out the upstairs," I said.

"I'm right behind you."

The wrought iron stairway groaned as we ascended. The top opened up to a short hallway with doors to two rooms on each side. My neck hairs told me to turn around and go back downstairs. Instead, leaning my rifle against the wall, I pulled my Luger and reached to the side to turn the first room's doorknob. No sound – so far so good.

I pushed the door fully open and stormed into an empty room containing a double bed covered by a handmade quilt. The closet was filled with frilly, flowery housedresses and sensible shoes. The walls were garnished with framed photos of unique flowers. A Singer treadle sewing machine with chair filled one corner next to an Art Deco waterfall dresser with a round mirror and Bakelite handles on the drawers.

"I told you she was sweet," Nick said.

I reached under the pillow on one side of the bed and removed a sharp stiletto.

"But I could be wrong."

We stepped back into the hall and I repeated my movement on the next door. As soon as my hand touched the knob, a loud shot sounded and a hole the size of my head appeared in the door. Luckily, I had been standing to the side.

I kicked the wounded door wide and fired at the figure standing in the room. Gloved hands opened and a short-barreled shotgun dropped to the floor, followed by the friendly bartender from the prior night's patio party.

"That reminds me," Nick said. "I could use a beer."

"Maybe later. You can check the refrigerator when we go back downstairs."

I kicked the shotgun away from the dead man's hand – just in case.

The office room contained filing cabinets and a desk, which supported an electric lamp, a typewriter and a variety of Hummel figurines. There were strange squiggles drawn on the desk blotter as well.

"What are these little sculptures?" Nick asked.

"They're figurines that are quite popular in Germany," I said.

"Wasn't LaFond raised in Argentina?"

"I believe both countries enjoy some of the same marching

tunes."

"Should we check a few of these cabinets for information?"

"We'll let Donovan know about them. If he thinks they're important, he can send in a few feds to review their contents. Let's clear the next two rooms and then go back downstairs."

"Yeah. To the refrigerator."

I walked back into the hall and took one step when the far door on the left flew open and a screaming Arab with a Luger ran toward us firing his pistol. I fell back into the office, did a complete backward somersault, returned to the doorway in the prone position and fired my Luger at the attacker. I hit him in the right wrist, knocking the gun out of his hand, and in the left hip. He tumbled to the hall floor.

I could say that I leaped right on top of him. But actually I ran toward him, tripped on his Luger and landed — you guessed it — right on top of him. I gripped his right arm where my bullet hit him. He snarled in my face and, with his left hand, pulled a long curved knife out of his scabbard and tried to slice me in the neck.

At one time, that fanatic had of have worked in a sleazy neighborhood saloon, I thought. Because he kept yelling something about an "alley" and a "back bar." That didn't make sense to me.

Anyway, I blocked his stabbing attempt with my right elbow; then followed through by smashing my forearm into his nose. He choked. We struggled for the knife, which somehow ended up perforating the low-center area of his chest. Blood actually sprayed out of him for a couple of seconds while he went limp.

I got to my feet and heard a thumping sound coming from the room where the former saloon worker had been. I kicked the door inward, fully prepared to aerate another robed enemy.

The room was a mess of scattered trash, turned over chairs and broken beer bottles. The sound was coming from under a green tarp in the corner. Nick rushed over and lifted an edge of the covering.

"It's that Little goliath!" he exclaimed.

"Huh?"

"Penrod Little," he explained, "the gigantic, short-tempered fed!"

Yanking the canvas back, I saw the big State Department

official struggling against his bonds. He was bound and gagged and looked pretty upset. Bruises adorned his face. One eye was swollen closed. And blood soaked his jacket where he had apparently been shot, twice.

I cut the ropes and removed the gag. Little coughed, spit and cursed. His left arm hung useless where a bullet had destroyed his elbow. Another had neatly penetrated his lower right ribcage, only to leave a ragged, baseball size exit wound on his back.

He groaned like a grizzly as Nick and I sat the big guy up against the wall.

"Thanks, shorty," he said to Danby. "You and your boss came along at the right time."

"What happened to you?" Nick asked.

"I heard about the greenhouse from Misty. Thought I'd come over and check it out."

"Who did this to you?"

"That crazy cat lady shot me, and a couple of her Arabic-babbling servants dragged me up here for questioning!"

"Why, Penrod?" Nick chuckled, then said. "I can't help it. You got a funny name."

"And if I had one less bullet hole in me, runt, I'd throw you through a wall!" Little turned toward me. "There was no one in that lobby when I walked in, so I looked around. Eventually, I found the way to the greenhouse. I saw the gigantic cornstalks, the orchids and the twisted cotton."

"You were alone?"

"I thought so. Then I heard a squeal coming from a wood-sided room at the rear of the glass house. The door to the area was slightly opened. I walked to it and took a look inside. It was floor to ceiling giant plants, and they were moving."

"Moving?"

"Tendrils the size of giant octopus tentacles were reaching out, coiling and uncoiling. From a textbook I had seen once, I recognized a Venus flytrap; except it was big enough to be a Venus condor trap!"

I looked at Nick. "Your girlfriend has been experimenting on jungle carnivorous plants!"

"The room was packed with them!" Little continued. "And right in the middle was Dr. LaFond, laughing and talking to the monsters. She held a kitten in her left hand and cackled while she threw another into the gaping hole of an eight-foot-tall plant that looked like a big pair of red lips!

"I thrust the door wide open so some of the kittens on the floor could escape. She turned toward me with her eyebrows arched, one eye closed and the other open enough for two, and shrieked. I started to make my escape when she reached under her apron, pulled a pistol out of her flowery dress and blasted me. I assume it was due to the smell of my blood, but one of those plants leaned in my direction and dripped green saliva from its hell hole!"

"You know," Nick said. "If Big Jim ever offers me another little vacation on the taxpayers' dime, I'm gonna join the Army. It's safer."

"So how'd you get up here?" I asked.

"The bullets knocked me back into the door," Little said. "I used my legs to push my way out of that room. That evil woman stood over me, ready to finish me off when two Arabs arrived. One of them spoke a little English. I heard him tell her they had just come from what sounded like 'poppy fields' and that someone was loading a plane. She ordered the men to take me upstairs and interrogate me."

"I'll bet the stairs were a bit rough."

"Those robed assholes were breaking their backs until the stupid bartender showed up and helped them. Anyway, they did their jobs trying to beat information out of me. Luckily, I didn't know anything about their activities or, apparently, yours."

I went to the bathroom and retrieved a couple of towels, which I used to clean his wounds and pack the one on his back to slow down the bleeding. Then, it took a while to get him on his feet and help him downstairs. He sat down on the couch while Nick and I inspected the greenhouse. Everything looked familiar until we reached the special room in the back. It was exactly as Penrod Little had described, minus the crazy cat lady. The barely moving monstrous carnivorous plants seemed sated, their bellies having been filled with scrumptious feline delicacies.

The floor was littered with slimy blue collars that obviously had been regurgitated. I reached down, fetched one, wiped it off on a piece of soiled canvas and stuck it in my pocket.

"Let's get Penrod back to the hacienda," I said. "There has to be another doctor in that house besides the cat killer."

"Yeah," Nick said. "But LaFond is still running loose."

"She's probably just whipping up some more cornbread for the visitors."

"Should we burn those gross plants, and this whole lab, to the ground?"

"We don't have time," I said. "That can be done later, once all the maniacal Arab drug dealers, mad scientists and enemy sympathizers have been rounded up. Besides, there are a couple of Remington paintings in the other room. Burning them would be a real crime!"

Because getting Penrod Little downstairs had been quite a handful, I had left my German rifle upstairs. Thinking as fast as I could, I made sure I had a full magazine in my Luger.

"C'mon, Nick," I hollered. "Let's get Mr. Little back to the hacienda. Nick? Nick? Where the hell are you?"

"Right here, boss," the single-minded chauffeur said, while coming out of the kitchen with three bottles of beer in his mitts. "I figured helping the big guy might be thirsty work."

He got no arguments, as the fed and I each accepted a brew and started stumbling to the front door. Once outside and on level ground, we were able to pick up a little speed. I knew Penrod was in quite a bit of pain, but he held up quite well.

We had almost reached the main building when we saw Hoot, Buck and Arlis Unger running toward us. The two cowboys stepped in to hold up Penrod. Unger checked the wounded man.

"There's a surgeon among the Chilean guests," he said. "Let's get Penrod inside one of the rooms and I'll fetch the doctor."

"On the bottom floor, please," Little said.

"We'll use the kitchen," Nick stated. "There's a clean table in there, as well as a few items the doc might be able to use."

"Yeah," an accusing Gibson said to Danby, "and beer in the fridge."

I looked at Hoot. "Did you find Misty?"

"No," he answered. "She's not in her room. We found Arlis in his, but Hunziger isn't around. Many of the guests are asleep, but a lot of them seem to be partying through the night."

"Okay," I said. "Nick, you and Arlis Unger stay in the kitchen with Penrod. Make sure he is patched up. And keep an eye out for the cat killer and Maria Dracula, or whatever her name is. Have you got ammunition?"

"I've got enough to take out those two black widows."

"Good. Hoot, Buck, let's get to the airport. Donovan and Crash may be needing our help."

We all worked together to get Penrod into the kitchen; then the three of us started for the stables. We noticed a bar had been set up outside near the patio entrance. Several men and women were drinking and laughing like it was New Year's Eve at Time's Square. A large sheet had been tied between two posts not far from the refreshment center. Several partiers were seated while an old silent western was being projected on the makeshift screen.

"Wow, look Hoot," Buck Jones said. "Isn't that you up there looking very heroic?"

"No, Buck," Gibson said. "That's Harry Langdon. I'm taller."

On film, the silent comic was riding in front of a small herd of cattle while attempting to roll a cigarette with one hand like William S. Hart.

"Hey," Jones stated. "It sounds like someone has added some sound effects to that flicker."

We stopped and looked up at the screen, as the noise became louder, sounding very much like a stampede. Then we saw the Rancho Grandé steers behind the screen kicking, snorting and thundering right at us, followed by a dust cloud that masked a giant shadow looming above the crazed bovines.

"What the heck?" Gibson spat, as a steer flew through the air above the projected film.

A large woman wearing an Austrian beer-garden waitress outfit tossed her tray of six full mugs of ale into the air, turned and slammed into the small table that held the projector, knocking it to the ground and ending the evening's motion picture presentation. The running, screaming audience members didn't seem to mind, in that the screen was being ripped in half by a thirty-foot centipede with half of a steer in its mouth.

"Take out the head!" I yelled, as the three of us pulled our weapons and began firing.

The creature spit the beef from its mouth and roared, while white liquid mixed with red blood drizzled out of its face. One of its eyes exploded, but that didn't seem to slow it down. It arched its neck like a striking rattlesnake and faced directly at us.

"Should we run?" Gibson asked.

"Won't help," I said. "Just keep shootin'!"

We heard the rifles firing from behind us. I dropped to one knee, turned and saw four vaqueros firing their M-1903 rifles from the prone position. They seemed to be targeting their .30-06 caliber rounds to the center of what could be described as the centipede's throat.

The beast roared one more time; its head rolled backward and its body went limp. We stepped back as the nightmare insect crashed to the ground. Instantly, the vaqueros rushed forward and used their machetes to behead the creature.

Needless to say, the outside partiers seemed to unanimously prefer taking their celebrating inside. I saluted the four vaqueros and continued our trek to the stables where four saddled horses stood nervously at the hitching post. We took three and followed the gravel road toward where I hoped we would find the airport.

CHAPTER 8. SEARCH AND DESTROY

As I rode, I thought about our situation. We were in Brazil, not Japan, Germany or Russia. Our enemies wore no uniforms and waved no flags. And although they received some financial support from the Fuhrer, the emperor and the soviet premier, they held no official alliances with any government. The one thing they had in common with their financiers was their hatred for America.

Although they lacked the military capability to launch an invasion or conquer territory, their sole purpose seemed to be an attempt to terrorize our civilian populace while destabilizing our economy and culture. And that thoroughly pissed me off.

Having been an infantryman in the Great War, I had hated the enemy. At the same time, I knew uniformed German soldiers were fighting for their country, just like me. Therefore, I also had respect for enemy troops. But Dom Sebastian, or whatever his name was, and his robed rogues were not uniformed military men. They were terrorists of the worst kind who didn't deserve to be called soldiers. The same could be said for Maria, the not-so-friendly late bartender, the crazy cat killer and any other disguised evildoers that happened to be attending Roosevelt's cowboy clambake along the Amazon.

I was beginning to think about what a long, tiring day and evening it had been when I noticed the slightest illumination growing in the eastern sky.

"Holy poop!" Gibson said. "That's morning headed our way! I missed my beauty sleep."

"From what I can see," I said, "you've missed that quite a lot over the last several years."

"Maybe we can get some coffee at the airport," the ever-optimistic Buck added.

We saw the glow of several torches as we advanced toward the ranch airfield. The dirt runway looked to be in very good shape. At the far end of that runway were what appeared to be the remains of a wooden barracks, like the ones I remembered from Fort Benning, still smoldering from a recent fire.

Where we arrived, a well-built modern control tower cast a morning shadow across three parked trucks and two biplanes. Next to them sat two large cargo planes, one was a DC-3 and the other a Douglas B-18 that looked suspiciously familiar. There seemed to be a lot of activity near one large well-lighted hangar with its big doors open.

We tied our horses to a post near the hangar and walked to the front where we could see what was going on inside.

"Hey, Curly. C'mon in. Bring your friends," the redheaded G-man said. "Even Hoot."

Several lanterns strategically placed on a few workbenches illuminated the interior of the hangar. Donovan and Crash stood smiling near their horses.

"Would you guys care for a beer?"

Smiling Bob, our federal pilot, walked from behind a shiny wood-sided Ford Station Wagon with a case of Mexican beer in his arms. Agents Long and Wagner sat on a bench sipping suds while holding their pistols on two leather jacket-wearing men who were sitting on the ground with their hands and feet tied.

"You were right about those truck drivers, Buck," Crash said. "They just wouldn't give up. We had to kill 'em."

"Rabid Moslem fanatics," Jones said. "You did them a favor. What about these two guys?"

"Can you believe they were part of the kitchen crew? Hans and Fritz were warming up our DC-3 out front," Slate said. "These schmucks were not only gonna steal our plane, but I'm sure they had plans to deliver opium and crazy bug fertilizer to a variety of places, including the United States."

"What's with the burning building at the other end of the field?" I asked.

"No idea," Donovan said. "It had just started flaming when we arrived. Not much left of it now."

I took a big drink of my breakfast beer and then got down to bringing Donovan, Crash and the feds up to date on our activities.

"I used the radio equipment in the tower to relay information home concerning our situation," Slate explained. "We have a small 'base' near Mexico City that is sending assistance."

"Marines? Bombers? Exterminators?" Hoot asked.

"A planeload of our secret special forces will arrive in the next twenty-four hours."

"And until then?"

"We round up all of our people and get the hell out of here!"

"Nick and Arlis Unger are taking care of Penrod Little," I said. "The big guy was wounded. Misty and Bill Hunziger are missing."

"Wagner, you and Long stay here," Slate ordered. "Keep the Katzenjammer pilots on ice and guard those planes. No one flies out of here until we get back. Bob, make sure our planes stay ready for takeoff.

"You cowboys mount up. I'll take the Ford. Let's go find our people!"

"Did I mention that Maria and Dr. LaFond are still loose?" I said.

"And they may not be alone," Hoot added. "These enemy assholes don't wear uniforms. Just about anybody we run into could be allied with the bad guys."

"Gee," Crash added. "The least they could do is wear black hats."

Hoot, Buck and Crash mounted up and started galloping back toward the hacienda. I jumped in the Ford passenger seat with Donovan behind the wheel.

"I'm worried about Misty," I admitted. "If Maria is half as evil as her fake brother, we still have a big job to do. And that Dr. LaFond definitely has bedbugs in her belfry."

"We'll search every inch of the property," Slate said through gritted teeth. "None of our people will be left behind."

The redheaded fed floored the gas pedal, which kicked up a dirt cloud that made me glad I hadn't mounted up for the ride. I believe I saw Hoot shaking his fist at us as we passed the three horsemen just before they vanished in the dust.

I thought about what we were facing. Following the centipede beheading, I didn't consider the vaqueros to be enemy. They were simply cowboys trying to protect the ranch. I hoped we could get them to help us find and rescue our people.

The fake Dom Sebastian must have kept his heroin security limited to fellow Moslems. Yet, the late bartender was certainly a villain, and so were LaFond and Maria. And the two kitchen-worker pilots were German. At that time, trust was something that was certainly going to have to be earned.

My priority was going to be finding Misty.

****

The early morning sunlight cast surrealistic shadows across the carcass of the beheaded centipede, torn movie screen-sheet, crunched projector, toppled chairs, and bottles and beer mugs strewn across the hacienda yard. We parked near the patio entrance next to half of an unlucky steer.

"It looks like everyone is inside," Donovan said, as we climbed out of the Ford.

I heard the sound of hoofs pounding on the dirt road. The three white-hatted cowboys reined in their animals and dismounted next to our vehicle. Gibson made a point of using his bandana to wipe the dust off his face.

"What took you so long?" I asked.

"We had to stop," the facetious Hooter said. "My horse wanted his privacy while he made a pile of your favorite biscuits."

Crash looked confused while Buck just shook his head.

"Everyone be on guard," Donovan said. "We don't know what to expect. So keep your guns in your hands as we enter. And, once inside, spread out."

"Yeah," Gibson said. "If we're too close together, the sergeant says, one grenade could get us all."

"That sergeant was smarter than we thought."

We advanced across the tiles toward the entrance to the building. The door opened and a well-armed vaquero, holding his Springfield rifle in both hands, stepped out and faced us. He had a Luger on his hip, ammo pouches connected to his belt and a sling bag containing what looked like grenades.

"Senhor Buck," the Brazilian cowboy said. "The guests are inside. They are scared to death."

Jones smiled and faced the man. "You speak very good English. What is your name?"

"I am Paulo. I am Brazilian vaquero. I also speak Spanish."

"Wonderful," Jones said. "You can translate for us. We need to round up our fellow Americans. We also are on the lookout for Maria Sebastian and Dr. LaFond."

Paulo spit. "Dr. LaFond has poisoned the earth!"

"We know. And Maria is also behind the death and destruction that has befallen this rancho. We hope your vaqueros will join us in capturing those responsible and keeping everyone else safe."

"We will, Senhor Buck! We proud to fight alongside you, Senhor Crash and Froggy Millhouse."

Gibson started to say something, but I shushed him. "Who cares who they think you are?" I whispered. "We need their help."

Paulo led the way into the hacienda.

"Let's start in the kitchen," I said. "That's where we should find Nick."

We followed the vaquero through the pantry and into the hacienda's large kitchen. Seated around a fair-sized table covered with empty bottles were three men with suspiciously silly expressions.

"Hey, Curly, Hoot," Nick slurred. "Join the party."

Big Penrod Little smiled and, using his arm that wasn't in a sling, slapped his new best friend, Nick, on the back. "Yeah, c'mon in. The beer's fine."

"Uh, oh," Hoot said.

"Hi, Donovan, and you other guysh," Arlis Unger added. "Dr. Rojas fixed Penrod up jush fine."

"Yep," Little said. "Now he's out in the dining room patching cuts and bruises."

"I can see why Mr. Little might need some painkiller," I said to Nick. "But you aren't wounded – yet. And we've got a job to do."

"Don't be shilly," the tipsy chauffeur slurred. "I'm jober as a studge."

Ignoring the stumblebums, Buck took charge. "Paulo, lead the way into the dining hall. Crash, you and Penrod move to my left. Hoot, you take Nick to my right. Curly, you and Donovan head up the stairway. Arlis, stay behind me. All of you keep your eyes open for trouble."

The dining hall was packed with complaining guests – some in informal attire, a few wearing tuxedos and gowns, and a couple of guys in flannel pajamas. I recognized a few waiters and members of the kitchen crew, not fully uniformed for their job categories.

"Yeehaw!" Buck screamed, while waving his big white hat.

His audience turned quietly and faced him.

"Thank you. This is my friend Paulo. He is going to translate for me."

Immediately Paulo addressed the crowd, first in Portuguese and then in Spanish.

"Some of you saw the centipede. And I'm sure the rest of you were told about it."

Buck waited as Paulo explained.

"In order for everyone to safely get the hell out of here, we first must find out who's missing. So you need to gather together with the people from your contingent."

Paulo looked questioningly at Buck.

"I mean your group; representatives from Chile; representatives from Columbia; etc."

Paulo nodded and then interpreted the remarks.

"I would like all Americans to please come over to the corner near the kitchen door."

After the vaquero translated Buck's statement, I saw the gathering moving and, slowly, forming into individual clusters of guests. From my stairway vantage point, my eyes darted around the room below me. Misty wasn't in the assemblage.

But then, moving like a muskrat through reeds, a nasty little man scurried over to Buck. It was U.S. Sen. Ted Bilbo, Democrat of Mississippi, followed closely by Bill Hunziger.

Buck waved his hat again and the people returned their attention to the speaker. "Once you are together, take notice of anyone who is missing from your group and let us know."

Paulo repeated the instructions to a bunch of confused people. Most of them shook their heads. A chef walked to the vaquero and spoke to him, then returned to his group.

"It seems like everyone is here except for two members of the kitchen staff," Paulo reported.

"How about your vaqueros? Have you lost anyone?"

"No one other than Esteban, senhor. A few of us are patrolling the wall. Two men are stationed at the stables and one more is on the roof."

Cautiously, we all returned to the corner by the kitchen door.

Buck addressed the Americans. "Do any of you speak Portuguese or Spanish?"

Hunziger nodded. "I speak Spanish."

"Good. You will stay here with Penrod, Arlis and the senator, while Paulo joins the rest of us in our search efforts."

"No suh! Less go, cowboy!" the senator spat. "Screw these folks. We need to get outta heaw!"

"Not until we've found our missing State Department official, Arlene Mistevin," I said.

"Aw am a U.S. senator! We go now, boy!"

I turned toward Donovan, who shrugged and looked the other way as I bashed the Klansman in the face, dropping him on his federal ass and spreading his already bulbous nose up into the bags under his eyes.

"You just stay right there, Senator Bo Bo, or I will personally feed you to a thirty-foot centipede."

Nick began to giggle, until I snapped my angry expression around and faced him.

"Sober up, buddy! We're gonna turn this joint upside down and find Misty!"

"Many of the rooms will be locked," Paulo offered.

"Is there a sledgehammer available?"

"Give me a moment, senhor."

Paulo left the room quickly. Penrod used his good arm to pull up a chair and sit down. He then put one foot on the senator's chest and smiled. Unger and Hunziger also retrieved chairs, while ignoring the sputtering coming from the elected asshole.

"Nick," I said. "You're gonna stay here and take charge of these people. Keep our group together. Get the kitchen crew to round up some coffee and toast for everyone. And Paulo, if Nick even mentions the word 'beer,' you need to thump him!"

"With pleasure."

"Dom Sebastian's Shiite house has three floors," I said. "There are six of us – a squad. We'll start off together on the third floor. Our mission is to find Misty and then get everyone to the airfield safely. If we encounter any armed resistance, kill them! If we run into Maria, kill her! If Dr. LaFond shows up, kill her! Search and destroy!"

"Works for me," Donovan said.

Paulo returned with a stout sledgehammer.

****

The first thing we noticed when we stepped off the stairs onto the third floor was that the doors on all three of our rooms were open.

"Looks like someone else has been doin' a little searchin'," Jones said.

I advanced to the side of the open door with my Luger ready. Buck silently moved to the other side. I entered first, moving rapidly with my finger on the trigger.

The suite was empty. It looked like someone had checked the drawers and closet quickly, but nothing was missing.

Donovan and Hoot hit the next room while Crash and Paulo searched the third, finding the same situation.

We searched the rest of the third floor rooms. Some doors were unlocked. And the locked ones didn't put up much of a fight against Paulo's sledgehammer.

"So far, no cigar," Hoot said.

"Yeah," I responded. "It's time we split up. Donovan, take Crash and Buck to search the second floor. Can you handle things without a sledgehammer?"

"I have a little experience in kicking in locked doors."

"Good. Hoot. You and Paulo come with me down to the first. Anybody hear gunfire, come a-runnin'."

****

When we arrived at the bottom of the stairs, I saw a smiling Nick Danby standing behind a table that held a large metal coffee dispenser, rows of cups, trays of toast and open jars of jam. The goofy chauffeur waved at us while filling cups for the long line of guests and staff. Penrod was sipping a cup of java while seated with one foot still holding the schmuck senator on the floor under the disapproving glare of Bill Hunziger.

We quickly went into the kitchen and pantry, where we checked all of the large cupboards and refrigeration compartments. Then we moved to the hall and into another storage room that contained pots, pans and cooking utensils along with hampers and carts.

The more our searching endeavors came up snake eyes, the more I felt we were going to be too late to help Misty. How could a woman as beautiful as her just vanish without a trace? It didn't seem possible. But then again, it hadn't been that long ago that seven-foot opium poppies, giant centipedes and plants that ate cats also didn't seem possible.

We sledged our way into a few more rooms without learning a thing. I felt defeated as I stood in an opening facing the large courtyard where the party was held on our first night in the hacienda.

"Snap out of it, Curly," Hoot ordered. "Let's check this area for clues."

"Clues?" I thought to myself. "There's nothing down here but a bunch of potted trees and plants and that monstrous growling beaver water fountain."

The room looked different without any tuxedo and gown-wearing celebrants sipping booze and slapping backs. In fact, the emptiness gave the place a strange atmosphere of dread. I looked to the center of the patio and got a slight tingle from the hair on the back of my neck. The scaly, grizzly bear, beaver statue was there all right, but water was no longer flowing out of its fangs into a pond. The pond was dry. And something, other than the strange image itself, was odd about the beaver.

I walked to the stone bench where Misty and I had enjoyed our first conversations. I looked at the fountain and realized the statue was different. On the night of the party, the beast had been facing directly at our bench. That was no longer the case. It seemed to be facing slightly to my left toward where Penrod Little had dangled Nick.

"Over here, guys!" I yelled.

The circular base of the gigantic sculpture was just slightly moved so it didn't match up with the tile around it.

"Give me hand. Let's see if we can slide this rock beast!"

The sculpture slid very easily, exposing a circular opening.

"This thing isn't solid rock at all! It's light enough to be a hollow plaster beaver."

"And there's a ladder in that hole," Gibson said. "You should go down there and check it out."

"Yes, *we* will."

I went down the ladder to a floor approximately twenty feet below the entrance. Light from the patio exposed what looked like a large, damp basement area. Obviously, the fountain pond had been leaking into the lower level for quite some time.

I struck a match and walked to where I found a stack of torches leaning against a block of stone. I picked one up and set it ablaze, lighting up the large, rock-walled room, which looked to be at least thirty feet wide and one hundred feet in length. It was obviously a storage room, as it was filled with rows of wood boxes and stacks of bags.

"Paulo, toss me your rifle and then come on down. Leave your hammer by the beaver, in case Donovan checks things out up there."

I caught the vaquero's Springfield, and then his bag of grenades before he came down the ladder. Then, reluctantly, Gibson followed.

"There's not much down here but a bunch of boxes and bags," Hoot said, as he put a match to another torch.

"Yeah, bags of G-719 giant bug chow!" I said. "And those boxes are filled with large rolls of pure opium."

"And all of that couldn't have been brought here through the giant beaver opening."

We spread out with our backs against the wall at the end of the basement near the ladder, each of us with a torch in one hand and a pistol in the other. Paulo kept his rifle on a sling over his shoulder. I was in the center with Hoot to my right and Paulo to my left when I motioned to advance. From my path, I couldn't see over the boxes to where the vaquero was walking, but I could make out the light movement from his torch. Gibson's big white hat could be seen above the fertilizer bags to my right.

When we reached within twenty feet of the other end of the room, I got a view of an arched opening in the wall. Then I heard a scraping sound, something like fingernails on a blackboard, if they were attached to King Kong's hand.

"Whoa, Spark Plug! Did you see that?" Hoot ran forward, pointing at a long, black tube vanishing into the arched entryway.

"A giant rat's tail!"

"I don't think so, Hoot," I said. "It was hard and awkwardly bent, like a branch."

"Maybe the giant rat was dragging a club."

"Only one way to find out," I said, as I led the way into the arched tunnel.

We closed in together while we rushed into what looked to be a long, dark, brick archway with carefully carved keystones. The floor was dirt, with hot and cold running cockroaches, slugs and beetles.

"At least those slimy little creeps haven't been chowing down on the G-719," Hoot stated.

That's when we heard the scream of terror.

"Misty! We're here!" I yelled and started to run forward.

The ear-splitting sound of metal against stone reverberated throughout the tunnel as a large rusty-iron plate rolled out of the wall and closed off our retreat to the basement.

CHAPTER 9. BATTLE OF THE BUGS

The orange glow of our torches illuminated the brick walls, the moving swarm of insects on the floor and black smoke gathering above us.

"No!" a woman screamed. "Don't come this way, Curly!" It was definitely Misty.

An evil cackle echoed off the walls.

"That sounds like crazy Dr. LaFond!" I told Hoot. "Keep your eyes peeled. We're probably walking into a trap."

"Good to know."

"Paulo hand me one of those grenades."

I stuffed the frag into one of my shirt pockets. With my left hand holding a torch, I returned my Luger to my right.

The tunnel began to close in on us. Bricks were replaced by beam-supported dirt.

"It could be the lost Dutchman's mine," Gibson whispered.

The scraping sound began again as we reached a bend in the tunnel. I saw what looked like a giant rat's tail whip out of the darkness around the corner. It awkwardly thrashed at us, knocking Hoot to the ground. Immediately, Gibson was dragged deeper into the tunnel. Dropping my torch, I ran forward and dived on him, grabbing what felt like a wooden branch, except it throbbed like it was bark over muscles.

Hoot fired his pistol toward whatever was dragging us, with no effect. I shoved my pistol into my belt, gripped a grenade in my right hand, used my left thumb to pull the pin and tossed it toward the front as hard as I could, hoping whatever had us didn't pull us directly into the blast.

The explosion was deafening. A cloud of dirt, rocks and pieces of wood engulfed us. But we were no longer being pulled. Jumping to our feet, Gibson held his torch close to the thing that had his leg. Through the thick dust we could see it was some kind of branch, or root. The thing had been blasted into several pieces, all of which were twisting on the ground like a hacked up snake that wouldn't die.

The crazy woman's cackle filled our ears like curdled milk. "Your weapons might kill men," she screeched. "But my babies will just heal and continue to feed!"

I retrieved my torch as the dust settled. The flame's orange glow illuminated fibrous tentacles thrashing the air around us – all leading to a large, dark shape in the center of tunnel. The pieces of roots continued to flop around our feet like eels out of water.

"Holy hibiscus, Hoot," I alliterated. "That's one of the cat killer's colossal carnivorous creatures."

"That's easy for you to say."

Out of the darkness I could see the giant red lips dripping with green ooze at the center of the tentacle storm. All three of us began firing into the creature. Several holes appeared in the bark, only to close while the tentacles continued to advance around us. The unseen mad doctor cackled loudly at our futile attempts to kill the beast.

With the speed of a pit viper, one of the tentacles wrapped around my right forearm, squeezing tightly enough to cause me to drop my Luger. Instantly, I shoved the flaming end of my torch to the clutching root, which brought about a loud screeching howl from the beast. The root broke off a few feet from my arm as it burned like an oily rope. The end that was wrapped around my arm uncoiled and dropped to the ground before it flamed up and became the consistency of a burnt matchstick.

"That's it, men!" I yelled, while retrieving my Luger. "Use your torches on the roots. That thing is like kindling filled with flammable sap!"

We ran forward swinging our torches at the thrashing roots. The beast squealed like a losing politician on Election Day. Foul-smelling, greenish-gray smoke mingled with the torch soot that filled the tunnel. Yet we could see the flailing beast as it was baptized in blazing hell. The giant red lips opened and a death scream emerged and faded, replaced by flaming ashes from its dying entrails.

"C'mon!" I yelled, while rushing into the ash heap.

I kicked burnt matchstick tentacles and pieces of charcoal out of my way while we fought past the charred remains of the carnivorous creature. Once on the other side, we entered an immense, well-lighted underground chamber.

Standing directly in front of us was a human nightmare. Dr. Anita LaFond arched her back and screamed incomprehensibly. Her eyes bugged out farther than a giant spider's. Her mouth was open like a spitting cobra as she called us "monsters," "murderers," and "botanic butchers!" Her flowered dress and apron were torn and filthy.

Standing directly in front of us was a human nightmare.

Gibson and Paulo looked at me with question marks in their eyes. I knew my plan was to kill the crazy witch. (Notice how I cleaned that up?) But I felt some kind of pity for the doctor. And, I thought, we might be able to learn something from her. Therefore, I put a bullet in her kneecap.

You'd have thought I had destroyed her flowerbed by the way she screamed, as she dropped to the ground and flopped around. Her continued cursing was certainly not very ladylike.

"Curly! Over here!" Misty yelled.

At the far end of the cavernous underground chamber, I could see a row of cages. I ran toward the one that contained the most beautiful prisoner I had ever seen. Misty was still wearing riding boots, jodhpurs and a torn, streaked blue shirt. Her gorgeous face was smudged with dirt and her eyes flashed with excitement.

"Thank God!" she said from behind bars.

"Ditto."

There was a heavy metal lock on her cage door.

"Where's the key?"

"That witch has it!"

Gibson was able to retrieve a key from the whiny botanist's apron. I opened the cell gate and Misty and I embraced each other tighter than root tentacles. Following a short time, and Hoot clearing his throat, twice, we stepped apart and smiled.

"How'd you end up here?"

"Nick had gone to the outside bar to get a couple of beers and I thought it would be good time to grab a sandwich. I entered the kitchen and noticed two white-shirted staff members staring at me. It made me nervous, so I started to leave. They grabbed me and covered my mouth with a cloth. It obviously had contained ether. When I woke up, I was in here."

"Where's that nasty Maria Sebastian woman?" I asked

"I don't know. But I do know where Dom Sebastian is."

"Yeah. He's dead."

"No, He's right over there!"

Misty pointed to a cage set back into the shadows. I walked over and saw an old man seated on a pile of rags, wearing tattered clothing.

"That's the real Dom Sebastian," she said. "He's been locked up down here for the last three years, while that self-dubbed sheik and his fake sister portrayed the patrons of the land."

"Why didn't they just kill him?"

The old man lifted his head and smiled. "Periodically, they need my signature. They fired, and killed, most of my staff. Then they hired new people of questionable backgrounds who either didn't know or didn't care that they were fakes."

I turned back to Misty. "Why didn't they kill you?"

"I assume, initially they thought I might be of value as a hostage. But I figured my time had just about run out before you arrived."

I used the key to open Sebastian's cage. Hoot stepped inside to help him to his feet.

"We've got to get you both out of here, now," I explained.

"Since we can't go back the way we came, let's see if the bat-feces crazy doctor can direct us," Hoot offered.

We walked to the writhing nutcase in the apron.

"How do we get out of here?" Gibson asked.

"I'll never tell," she shrieked.

I pointed my Luger at her head.

"Hold on, Curly," Misty said with her hand on my arm. "You can't just kill her. She obviously has a mental problem. She needs help."

"So do we! And she's a dangerous nut!"

"She's just a scientist who's made mistakes," Misty pleaded. "She likes plants. We should bring her with us."

I reached into my pocket and produced the baby blue kitten collar and handed it to Misty.

"Oh, my. That's Denny's. Where did you find it?"

"It had been regurgitated onto the floor in a room full of her giant carnivorous plants. One of that scientist's 'mistakes' was using kittens as plant food."

Misty froze. Her face became stoic as she clenched her teeth and, with lightning speed, grabbed my Luger from my hand and pumped four rounds into Dr. LaFond's chest.

"If you were trying to hit her heart, you probably failed," Gibson said. "I don't believe she had one."

"This way," the real Dom Sebastian said, hobbling toward the rear of the chamber. "There's a large entryway at the top of the incline."

The ground sloped upward at the far side of the chamber. Although it was a dirt floor, it was solid and looked like it could support a truck, if needed. We advanced until we arrived at a board and bat wood wall.

"Grab it at the base and lift," the old man said. "It will tilt up like a garage door."

The opening allowed us into a dark area filled with baled hay.

"This is the back of the stables," Sebastian said.

All of the stall doors were open.

"Where are my Campolinas?" he asked.

"Perhaps the vaqueros have them," I explained. "They are patrolling the area to keep out the big bugs."

Paulo nodded.

"We need to get back to the hacienda," I said. "We'll get our groups ready to travel to the airport, so we can all get the heck out of here."

I opened a sliding barn door at the front of the stables only to be knocked flying by a big white steer that ran into the structure. I looked out the door and saw a daylight nightmare that, had Hieronymus Bosch been into animal illustrations, he might have painted. Steers and horses were running in every direction, pursued by giant centipedes, scorpions, spiders and at least one stinkbug.

All of our eyes widened as we saw a fifteen-foot, red-lipped carnivorous plant loping along on multiple roots as it chased a horse. It sent a whip-like tentacle to snatch the Brazilian Campolina, only to be grabbed and tossed onto its back by a goliath banana spider. Both monsters reared onto their hind "legs" and roared at each other. In a move that made me wonder if the spider had ever seen Man Mountain Dean in action, the arachnid dived on top of the big-lipped plant, sinking its teeth into the beast's trunk.

If the plant could laugh, it probably did as it wrapped multiple roots around the big black, eight-legged, furry, venomous creature and crushed it like a grape. It then shoved the pulpy remains of the late web spinner between its lips while a scorpion rushed past with a steer in one of its claws.

"Maybe we should go back to the cages," Gibson said, in his inside voice.

"No. We've got to get to the hacienda," I said. "Once we're inside, we'll be safe."

Sebastian, Misty, Hoot and Paulo all looked at me as if my next words would tell them how we were going to do that. I was at a loss.

"I'm open to suggestions."

Paulo smiled, held up an index finger and then ran back into the stables. Within a minute, he returned with a flaming torch in his hand. He pointed at the torch and then at the plant devouring the spider.

"I get it!" I said. "A distraction."

"Yes, senhor," the vaquero said, as he started running toward the feasting, bark-covered meat eater.

"When that thing lights up, all hell is gonna break loose."

"It's already broke loose, Curly," Gibson said.

"As soon as the plant bursts into flame, run!"

Paulo was a pretty swell runner. He was almost to the gluttonous weed when a Duesenberg-sized stinkbug turned toward him.

"Hurry up!" Misty yelled.

It sounded like heavy bug breathing when the big black beetle lifted its shelled tail and scurried toward Paulo, who was within twenty feet of his destination. The brave vaquero didn't see the steer leg sticking up out of the ground in his path. He tripped and fell to the ground; the torch flying out of his hand and landing just out of his reach.

"No!" Misty hollered, as the beetle stopped right over the man.

Hoot and I started shooting, which is probably what we should have done sooner. Holes and rips appeared where our slugs perforated the stinkbug. It staggered to one side, lifted three legs in the air and fell over, all the while emitting a thick, white liquid onto Paulo. The vaquero took his chance and jumped forward, picked up the torch and threw it onto the flammable flora. The creature burst into a tank-size orange and green flame, radiating bizarre shadows outward from the surrounding insects.

Steers don't like fire. Neither do bugs. The insects and their bovine prey all ran toward the open field to escape burning, among other things. The horses, being faster than steers, had already vanished from the scene. At the same time, Hoot and I each grabbed one of Sebastian's arms and started running toward the hacienda with him held high between us, and Misty leading the way.

Two Springfield carrying vaqueros covered us as Donovan held open the entrance into building. Once everyone was inside, a vaquero slammed down a bolt locking the door. Paulo and his two friends greeted each other warmly. Donovan slapped my back. "You found her! That's great, Curly!"

"She had been caged up in a cellar. Did you see the beaver statue entrance?"

"Yeah. Your sledgehammer brought us to it. That's a lot of bad stuff kept down there. But we didn't see any cages."

"Did you find a rusty metal wall?"

"Yeah."

"Cages are on the other side."

We walked back toward the formal dining room. Gibson leaned over to the white grease-covered Paulo and whispered, "You might want to take a quick shower."

"Yes, senhor Froggy. I stink."

"By the way, Donovan, this is the real Dom Sebastian," I said. "Dom, this is G-man Donovan Slate."

"I thank all of you," Sebastian said. "Not just for saving me, but for ridding Rancho Grandé of that evil man and his insane followers."

"We're not out of the hot water yet, sir," Donovan warned. "We have to get everyone to safety."

"I have another priority," Gibson announced as we entered the crowded dining room. "It's been a while since we've had any sustenance. I need a beer and a sandwich, in that order."

"I can take care of that," a smiling Nick Danby said. "C'mon, Arlis. Let's go make these folks some sandwiches. The beer will be right up."

Unger smiled and greeted Misty, then followed Nick into the kitchen.

"Mission accomplished?" Penrod Little asked, still keeping one foot on the bigmouthed senator.

"Yep," I answered. "So far so good. Think you'll be okay for a little air travel after a while?"

"No problem. But can we leave the senator here? He's an

idiot."

"Now Penrod. You've worked for the federal government for quite a while. He's not the only turd elected to that punchbowl. Don't you think Bilbo's peers might miss him?"

Little looked down at the bruise-faced man on the floor and said, "No. I don't."

Nick rushed back into the room with a tray of bottles of beer. He gave the first two to Misty and me. The considerate chauffeur had already removed the lids.

"Let's find a quiet spot and talk," I said to the gorgeous blonde fed.

We walked to an open couch where we sat down together. I had a thousand questions I wanted to ask her; but as soon as I looked into her eyes and she placed her electrically charged hand on my knee, I forgot what they were. She leaned in and kissed me on the lips. At that moment I knew I was very happy. I just didn't know who I was.

"You wanted to ask me some questions," she said in a voice that filtered down from the heavens.

"God yes!"

"What were they?"

"What were what?"

"Your questions."

"Can I have another kiss?"

CHAPTER 10. ESCAPE

"I know we had planned to get our people out of here," I said. "But we can't leave the others."

"I'm afraid you're right," Donovan agreed. "It's probably another dozen hours before our special forces arrive. By then, the insects will have probably finished off the steers and will start dismantling the hacienda in search of food."

"Yeah Curly, your crop fires and the destruction of the back gate has turned Rancho Grandé into a real bug buffet," Nick added.

"We've got the B-18 and the DC-3," I said, ignoring Nick's criticism. "Bob's still at the airport. Donovan, who're the pilots that flew your plane?"

"That was Stan Lingle and Sullivan Hanks. But I haven't seen them since we arrived."

"I have a feeling those Hans and Fritz guys may have taken them out for a bite with some of LaFond's dancing herbs," Nick said.

"Buck can pilot the DC-3, with Hoot as a just-in-case-of-emergency copilot," I said. "Bob can handle the B-18, if you ration out the beer."

"Don't worry about Bob," Donovan added. "I'll spell him whenever he needs a nap."

"Good. That takes care of the transportation for four pilots and about sixty passengers," I said. "The unfortunate thing is, I estimate approximately close to eighty people, including vaqueros, are in need of escape. And, you'll have to toss all unnecessary items out of the two aircrafts to get into the air with thirty passengers each."

"Even the parachutes?" Nick asked.

"Yep," I said. "But don't worry, Nick. You and I have other plans."

"Oh, shit."

I sat down with Buck and Hoot and explained the situation. After a few moans, groans and whines, I was able to explain that their country needed them. They were being drafted to fly the DC-3. "So try and stay halfway sober."

Then I asked Donovan if he had radio contact with Long and Wagner at the airport.

"I do. The radio is in our armoire under my tuxedo."

"Good. I want them, with the help of Bob, to take the three large trucks and unload piles of G-719 and boxes of opium at about every twenty yards around the perimeter of the runway. Just before you take off, those piles need to be doused with fuel and torched. The fires will keep the bugs away while destroying all of that poison."

"What'll they do with Hans and Fritz while they're driving around?"

"You know, those two fine specimens of National Socialism would be considered unnecessary weight on the airplane."

"Roger. Wilco."

"Come to think of it, if you tie them up very securely, they could be left in the hangar," I said, after feeling a twang of guilt. "If they survive the bugs until our special forces arrive, it'll be up to the uniforms as to what to do with them."

"How are we gonna get the passengers to the field?"

"As soon as your feds unload those trucks, they need to drive to the hacienda," I said. "Along with the Ford, they should be able to transport all of your passengers to the airfield."

Donovan went upstairs to contact Long and Wagner. I gathered the rest of the Americans, as well as Paulo and Dom Sebastian, together for beers and discussion. Nick, as usual, made sure there were enough cold bottles available.

"But why do Hoot and Buck get to fly the DC-3?" Corrigan asked. "I've got a pilot's license too."

"I didn't know that," I responded. "But think about it. The passengers are already scared to death. If they found out their pilot was named Corrigan, they'd worry they might not be going the right way. Then if someone explained to them that you weren't Wrong Way Corrigan, but that your name is Crash Corrigan, things could go south."

The ex-Mesquiteer grumbled and picked up a beer. I had to get everyone to understand how important it was to work as a team. Our lives depended on it.

"Paulo. You need to explain to the other guests that, once the trucks arrive, they will have to climb in them to get to the airport. Once there, Donovan will make sure they all are able to board the planes. Hopefully, we'll all be leaving in about an hour and a half."

Paulo explained to one group at a time that they needed to prepare to leave. Most of the people seemed happy about that. Some weren't thrilled with leaving their luggage in the hacienda.

"Dom Sebastian. You, Penrod, and Misty will ride to the airport in the Ford Station Wagon with Buck, Donovan and Hoot."

"I'm going with you!" Misty said, with a look on her face that told me not to argue.

"Okay. Arlis. You're in the Ford. Hunziger. I'm putting you in charge of Senator sheethead the Klansman. You'll both ride in the back of one of the trucks. Once you get to the airfield, follow agent Slate's orders."

"Y'all are gonna rue the day..." the flap-mouthed fool started to sputter, until Penrod thumped him on the forehead.

"Can't we leave him for the bugs?" Little asked.

"Nope."

"Well," Nick scratched his head and grinned like Stan Laurel, "that just leaves Crash, Misty, you and me."

"It certainly does," I said. "But don't forget Paulo and about a half dozen other vaqueros."

"So what do we do? Pretend this is the Alamo?"

"We're going to engage in a little arson and then go on a nice riverboat cruise. You may now refer to me as Captain Huckleberry."

"That's not exactly what I was thinkin' of callin' you."

Dom Sebastian had told me that there was a riverboat, which periodically brought supplies up the Amazon to various villages and plantations, and then carried cotton, corn and rubber back down the river to Manaus, and eventually to the Atlantic Ocean for international shipment. And that if we could get to a tribal village not too far away from the ranch, along the river, we may be able to hitch a ride.

112

He said there was a dirt landing field outside of Manaus where we could meet up with air transportation for our final exit from the jungle. Donovan just had to make sure an airplane would be waiting for us when we got there. I explained this to my friends when the suspicious chauffeur asked, "Is this where you get to say, nothing can go wrong?"

We all had enough time to go to our rooms, shower and get into clean clothes for the trip. When we returned downstairs, Nick had made sure sandwiches were available in the dining room. Misty and I grabbed beers to go with ours as we chuckled and talked about everything except the reality we were experiencing. Hoot and Crash had apparently buried the hatchet and were trading funny stories about various filming adventures. Buck sat in a corner while finishing his Raymond Chandler novel. Everyone at the ranch seemed to be in a giddy mood; obviously glad to be ready to leave while keeping their minds in denial of the fact that beyond the hacienda walls, the environment had become extremely deadly.

A vaquero rushed in from the patio waving his rifle.

"That's the signal. The trucks are coming. Line up, but stay in your own groups."

Paulo translated my words as an excitement rumbled through the room. The vaquero and I muscled our way to the front and looked outside. There were no bugs in sight, but that didn't mean they weren't there. I directed the three trucks to back up to the outdoor patio area. The vaqueros set up a perimeter, aiming their rifles outward while in the kneeling position. Once the line made it outside, Paulo and I split the passengers into three lines to board the trucks.

Donovan climbed behind the wheel of the Ford Station Wagon as Buck sat down next to him in the passenger seat. Hoot and Penrod squeezed into the middle seat and Arlis and Sebastian sat in the back. I motioned for Donovan to wait a moment, while I ran to a pillar and grabbed two beautiful Frederic Remington paintings.

"Hoot. Would you and Buck take good care of these until you get them home to America? Perhaps Big Jim could find a nice museum that would be pleased to have them."

"Sure thing, Curly. I just wish you were comin' with us."

"We'll see each other back in the good old red, white and blue, that is if Donovan sends a plane to pick us up in Manaus."

"Trust me," Donovan said, sporting his least sincere smile.

"Now get goin'! Put these folks on the planes, light the fires and grab some clouds. And try not to breathe any of that opium smoke."

Donovan hit the gas, getting the Ford on the way. One of the trucks had finished loading by then and moved in right behind the car. It only took a few minutes to load the other two trucks and get them on the road.

I waved for Paulo and the vaqueros to follow me as I ran into the now almost empty hacienda. Nick stood at the entrance wearing his chauffeur's cap and uniform, a pistol belt with a Luger and ammo pouches, a bayonet sticking out of the top of his boot, a canvas canteen on a sling and he was carrying a Springfield rifle. Cowboy Crash was also well armed with a two-gun belt and another rifle. Misty wore her small black western hat, jodhpurs, riding boots and a clean white blouse along with a six-gun strapped to her leg and several ammo pouches and a military canteen on her belt.

I was already wearing my new Luger shoulder holster over my shirt and had several loaded magazines shoved in my jacket pocket.

"Grab your torches, gang! Let's light this place up!"

Crash and Nick ran through the dining room, setting furniture, drapes and wall coverings on fire. Misty, Paulo and I headed to the stables first and then the deadly greenhouse. It didn't take long for all of Rancho Grandé's structures to become a giant funeral pyre for the evil that was created there.

Three vaqueros signaled for us to join them near the large metal gate that we had entered through the first night we arrived. They had opened the gate and were waiting with Nick and Crash as we ran toward them. I was shocked when I saw all of them drop to their knees and started firing at us. "What the hell, you guys?"

Paulo nudged me and I turned to see what he wanted. The greenhouse structure was blazing extremely bright and two goliath carnivorous plants stood on the porch, slashing their flaming tentacles in the air. "Good," I thought. "Burn you monsters!"

But that wasn't what the cowboys were shooting at. A centipede not quite the size of a General Pershing Zephyr streamliner was pushing its way out of the ground from under the flaming stables. I crouched and began firing at the head. Once again, it seemed like the vaqueros were concentrating their fire on the area, just below the head.

The creature thrashed its body in every direction while it roared and spewed green and orange slime into the air. With one last surge, it stretched straight up toward the sky and then dropped back into the burning stables. The vaqueros cheered and we all ran out the large gate and into the jungle.

For the first twenty minutes we continued to run, even though the foliage fought us all the way. When we stopped, we looked back into the evening sky and could still see the light from the ranch's flames and smell the smoke.

"Looks like things are going nicely at the airport as well," Crash said, pointing to another direction where a fiery glow reached up into the dusk.

"I hope so."

I checked my Tom Mix compass and then led the way toward the riverbank. The jungle was thick and dark, but it didn't have the ominous feeling that it had before. In fact, the farther away we got from Rancho Grandé, the less chance we had of running into big bugs. And that meant, the better off we were. Or so I thought.

"It's getting pretty dark, Curly," Misty said.

"And the jungle's beginning to make those creepy noises again," Nick added.

"Yeah, well we should arrive at the river in the next hour. And Buck said those noises are just a bunch of critters. Nothing to worry about."

"Didn't he say that about the time we ran into that first spider?" Crash asked.

"We can camp near the river. We'll have a fire and post guards around us. I think, with the vaqueros, we can each handle a few hours of guard duty and still get a bit of sleep."

"What about the Indians?" Crash asked.

"Sebastian told me the tribe that lives in our village destination is fairly friendly. The natives normally keep to themselves, but they trade with the outside world."

"When is our paddle wheeler scheduled to arrive?" Nick asked.

"That's the wild card. We don't know if the riverboat has made its run yet this month. If it hasn't, it could be anytime. If it has, well, there's always next month."

That stopped the questions. The darkness slowed down our progress while Paulo and the vaqueros hacked the brush in some areas so we could get through. We saw small snakes, small rats, and small spiders and scorpions no bigger than one's head – nothing to worry about.

The vaqueros smiled as we all felt the cool moisture of the river before we could see it. The Brazilian cowboys told us to wait as they scouted ahead to find a safe place to camp. Although their primary focus had been on handling ranch security and taking care of horses and cattle, those men had shown themselves to be seven of the toughest soldiers I had ever met. Our multi-lingual pal Paulo had become a fine leader for the group, all of whom had never batted an eye before taking on giant insects, securing a path through the jungle for a group of foreigners and following instructions given in the heat of bug battle. We couldn't have asked for better jungle escorts.

Misty snuggled up to my side and smiled into my eyes.

"You're a pretty serious man when you take charge," she said.

I smiled back. "Is that a good thing?"

"Couldn't be better."

Paulo returned and told us they had found a good spot to set up camp. We followed him to a somewhat clear area not too far from the river. The vaqueros were setting up a defensive perimeter.

"You don't want to be too close to the water," he said. "Many animals come to the river for water and food. And there are also black caiman in this area."

I asked and Paulo answered concerning the black caiman. After listening to a frightening description I realized the beasts were to crocodiles what Muscle Beach bullies were to ninety-pound weaklings. I took Misty's hand and led her to a nice bench-like log as far away from the river as possible.

Crash and Nick cleared an area for a campfire and went about gathering kindling and thicker branches. Some vaqueros used flat bases of dry palm fronds to dig foxholes while others gathered rocks to place in front of their defensive positions. I inspected my Luger and eyed the riverbank.

About the time Crash got the kindling burning and the vaqueros tossed their makeshift shovels into the fire, which blazed up not quite as brightly as a flaming carnivorous plant-monster. Although the temperature was not chilly, the fire's warmth offered comfort to our exhausted gathering. Nick continued to collect a fairly large pile of firewood to periodically add to the flames through the night.

Paulo tossed a small canvas bag in front of me.

"It's just biscuits and a couple of cans of beans," he said.

"Thank you, Paulo," Misty said. "You've been just wonderful."

"My men all brought their own biscuits. Be sure and don't crush or throw away the bean cans."

"Why's that?" Crash asked.

"Your two canteens should serve the four of you well," he answered. "But in the morning, you will want to refill them. Use the cans to boil river water before putting it in your canteens."

"Makes sense," I offered. "I'll bet there's some nasty things in that water."

"Yeah," Nick said. "Like piranhas."

"There are many kinds of piranhas in the Amazon River," Paulo stated. "Most of them are not man eaters. The main ones you need to worry about are the red-bellied piranhas."

"What kind do you think is out there right now?" Nick asked.

"Oh, probably the red-bellied kind."

"He sounds a lot like Buck," Crash said.

"Any information that keeps us alive is good information," I said.

The biscuits were good. The canteens were passed around. We ate the beans cold, rinsed out the cans and boiled river water in them to refill our canteens.

"Now, young lady," I said to Misty. "You should get some sleep."

I took off my jacket and placed it over her, while removing my Luger magazines and shoving them into my shirt pockets.

She snuggled close. "What about you?"

"I'm goin' to be on guard for three hours," I said. "Nick agreed to take the second three and Crash will wake up for the third. Paulo and his vaqueros will also spell each other at their perimeter positions."

"I should also take a turn at guard," she said.

"No need. By the time Crash finishes his duty, the sun should be beginning to rise," I said, while standing up and backing away from the fire. "I'll join you in just a little bit."

The fire was a good deterrent for jungle cats, crocodiles and any other creatures that might have planned to do their evening riverside business in our area. There was plenty of other riverfront space that would suffice for their needs. And I was pretty sure we were far enough away from Dr. LaFond's bug factory to be safe from attacking giant insects and weeds. But, even so, the fire would send a nice message. Now, if we were in a military situation with an enemy in the jungle, obviously we would not have used a fire. But, at that time, our perceived enemies all had four legs, claws, fangs and no political ideology.

I pulled my Luger from my shoulder holster so I could be ready for anything, and then leaned against a tree. The vaqueros were chatting among themselves; some of them were smoking some kind of rolled up leaf. Paulo walked the perimeter, inspecting their foxholes. An already snoring Crash Corrigan had found a soft sandy spot to curl up in next to a thick-leafed shrub with orange tubular flowers. Nick leaned against the backup firewood and watched the campfire's flickering red, yellow and sometimes blue flames.

The sleeping Misty was a glowing vision of loveliness. The more I looked at her, the more I saw her as a model in an Alberto Vargas painting. I rubbed my eyes, shook my head and looked away. When one is on guard duty, one should concentrate on possible threats, not beautiful blondes.

The rippling current of the river, the slight wave of the jungle trees in the breeze, and the almost musical sounds of the night impressed upon me what a unique and wonderful environment we were experiencing. Mother Nature certainly knows what she's doing, I thought, whether it is in the rainforests of Brazil, the redwoods of northern California or the Painted Desert and Grand Canyon of the Great Southwest. Dr. LaFond was a fool to want to tinker with perfection. And although I was thousands of miles from Hollywood, at that moment I felt I was home.

My three hours passed pleasantly. I awakened Nick for his tour on guard at midnight. Then I snuggled down next to the amazing Arlene Mistevin and, quickly, fell asleep.

****

I felt the warmth of the sun on my body as I sat up on the beach blanket and put one bare foot on the soft sand. The bright green waves splashed onto the shore not twenty feet from our blanket. The sounds of the seagulls garnished the beautiful afternoon, as I looked down at the lovely blonde bathing beauty leaning against our solar umbrella.

"Spack!"

Someone ran past our blanket and kicked sand at us.

"Hey! Keep your sand out of our faces!" I yelled.

The eight-foot black caiman in swimming trunks put his hands on his hips and frowned down at me. He opened his large, fang-filled mouth and, in a voice that sounded suspiciously like Flip the Frog, said, "What're you gonna do about it, shrimp?"

"Yeah," the blonde-wigged, Betty Boop bathing beauty said. "What're you gonna do, Curly?"

The ugly reptile slammed out the palm of his claw and knocked me onto my butt. "He ain't gonna do nothin'!"

Betty threw her banana daiquiri in my face, hooked arms with the overgrown water lizard and walked away.

I knew I had to do something. But what could I do?

I reached into my swim trunks and removed my Springfield M-1903 rifle and sent a .30-06 caliber round into the back of the caiman's head. Then I jacked another round into my rifle, took aim at Betty, and..."

"Wake up, sleepy head," Misty said. "It's a beautiful morning."

"I hate Betty Boop!"

"I'm more of a Daffy Duck fan, myself," she said. "Would you like a biscuit?"

I grumbled incomprehensibly until she took my head in her hands and kissed me on my lips. That electrifying coupling energized my being to point that I felt like I had just finished my third cup of coffee to find out my horse, Spark Plug, had defeated Seabiscuit in the Santa Anita Handicap.

"Good morning, dear," I sang. "It is a gorgeous morning."

"I'll have what he's having," a bleary-eyed Nick Danby said while on his way to answer nature's morning call.

We all took our time visiting various jungle plants that needed watering, gathering our weapons and supplies and preparing to continue our trek. I sprinkled a little tooth powder on my brush and scrubbed my teeth as best as I could, field style.

"How much farther to the village?" Crash asked.

"According to what Sebastian had to say, I'd estimate two to three hours of following the river."

"Piece of cake," Nick added.

"I wonder how Buck, Hoot and the others are doing," Crash said.

"I would guess that they would be arriving in Lima, Peru, within the next couple of hours. And I'd bet the forces being sent from Mexico are arriving at the remains of Rancho Grandé about now."

"Do you think they'll be surprised by their reception?"

"Nope. Donovan, I'm sure, would have been able to radio communications from the B-18 to someone who could have updated the troops to our plans. But they'll still have one hell of a mop-up mission on their hands."

Paulo motioned that his vaqueros were ready to hit the trail. I signaled back and Crash, Nick, Misty and I stepped right into the line, Army patrol style. Paulo led the way followed by three vaqueros, then us, then three more of his cowboys. The communal mood was far lighter than the previous day. After all, I was told the village was a friendly tribe, our friends surely must have escaped, the riverboat couldn't reject us and Misty was holding my hand as we walked. Life was good.

The air was humid along the riverbank. Every now and then I would hear a splash from one of those caimans entering the water or a squeal from a howler monkey. Apparently, we were irritating some of the local residents. A jungle cat roared in the distance, probably letting us know that we should keep moving. Anyway, the next few hours went by without too much excitement, until we got within a couple of hundred feet of our destination village.

The Indians had thinned the trees to build their homes near the riverbank. The structures had peaked roofs made from woven palms. The wooden walls were open above three feet to let air flow through the rooms. Every building was set on stilts where floors were seven feet off the ground. Like open garages, the spaces below the floors were used to store thin wooden boats. From our vantage point, the village looked attractively picturesque, except for one thing. There were no people.

"Hold up," I said, quietly. "Something's wrong here."

I looked at the open shore and the long, empty dock that obviously was built to accommodate a paddle wheeler. Next to that dock was a tall stack of firewood to be used in a steamboat furnace. The grounds were devoid of natives and it didn't look like anyone was occupying the buildings.

"Paulo," I said. "Have four of your men take Misty and Nick back into the jungle a ways. Then you, me, Crash and two vaqueros will advance and check out that village."

"Nick. Find a defensive site, hunker down and keep quiet." I turned to Misty. "Once we figure out what's happened here, we'll come back and get you."

We advanced on line, spread apart five yard from each other, into the village. What wasn't visible from a distance became glaringly apparent up close. The dock, the buildings and the grounds around the village were littered with the three Bs – brass, bullet holes and blood.

CHAPTER 11. RIVER OF DEATH

We searched the buildings, the boats and surrounding area thoroughly and the only living creatures that we could find were the flies that swarmed pools of dried blood. As the day warmed up, the smell increased. Our friendly village of Amazon Indians had turned out to be the site of a mass murder.

The sound of coughing and gagging caused me to turn to one of the huts where I saw Crash losing his morning biscuits over a railing. The only thing he could say was, "Cradle."

"But there are no bodies!" I said. "Where the hell are the dead?"

Paulo put one hand on my shoulder and shook his head.

"The river, senhor," he said. "The villagers were murdered and thrown to the sharp teeth in the water."

Whoever the fiends were that perpetrated the atrocity had help from their brethren, crocodiles and piranhas, in disposing their victims.

I looked at Paulo. "Was it bandits? Another tribe?"

"No, senhor. There are no bandits this far back in the jungle. If it were another tribe, there would have been a battle of arrows and darts."

"You're right," I thought out loud. "This was a precision military assault with the intention of annihilation. Probably done at night or early in the morning to catch these peaceful people off guard and in one place."

"By what I can see," Crash said, "this had to have taken place at least two days ago."

"Back when we were still fighting bugs and trying to find Misty," I said. "But who? And why?"

One of the vaqueros stepped up to us and conversed with Paulo in Portuguese for close to a full minute. Paulo then turned to me.

"There was a body found in the brush," he said.

"A villager?"

"No. It was a white man. He had apparently been wounded and had run as far as he could to escape the killers. He bled to death."

"A white man? What was he doing here?"

Paulo handed me the man's wallet and identification. I gasped. He was Edward Sanchez, captain of the Rio Amazon paddle wheeler.

****

We gathered together about six hundred feet from the village.

"This is horrible!" Misty exclaimed. "Who could do such a thing?"

"Monsters," I said. "Human monsters this time. From the trail of brass shell casings, it looks like a group of armed killers encircled the village and began shooting. The natives didn't have a chance. The trigger-happy bums closed in and blasted the structures, then went house to house killing everyone – men, women and children."

"But the boat captain...?" Nick asked.

"My guess is that Captain Sanchez had ventured into the jungle to relieve himself before the shooting started. He ran, was seriously wounded, but kept running. When he finally bled to death, he was beyond the reach of the killers."

"But why was he here?" Misty asked.

"We found recently delivered supplies stacked in one of the structures. I believe the riverboat arrived the evening before the slaughter. Supplies were unloaded and Sanchez and his crew decided to spend the night before going back down river."

"We missed the boat," Crash offered.

"We did. The killers didn't. Whoever butchered these people took the boat."

Nick stated the obvious. "And here we are, up the Amazon without a paddle."

"No, senhor!" Paulo said. "Come with me."

All of us scurried after the vaquero. He ran up in front of a line of huts on stilts.

"There's nothing in those buildings that can help us get to Manaus, Paulo," Crash said.

"Not in them. Under them."

We looked down to see that every structure had at least two tribal boats "parked" under the floors. They had been carved out of jungle tree trunks. And two wooden paddles were lying inside each boat.

"These boats can hold two people each," I said. "Six boats and we're on our way."

"You expect me to sit in one of these flimsy canoes just inches away from red-bellied piranhas and crocodilosauruses?" Nick sputtered.

"Well, yeah," I said. "Either that or you can wait here for a ride on a friendly giant stinkbug."

Standing there in his tattered gray uniform, the frowning chauffeur looked like a beleaguered Confederate troop, who in 1865 just realized he'd rather be a Yankee.

Crash and I gathered a couple of bags of canned beans and crackers from the supplies that the riverboat had delivered. We wrapped them in blankets and stored them aboard one of the boats.

"This is great!" Misty said. "It's just too bad we can't catch up with that riverboat and get even with those murderers!"

"Perhaps we can," I offered, as I took a swig from her canteen. "You remember that stack of firewood next to the dock. I'll bet alligators to anacondas the killers were in such a hurry to get out of here that they forgot to load their fuel."

"Yeah," Crash added. "That means they're gonna have to stop somewhere and cut their own supply of firewood. And that could really slow them down."

That explanation seemed to make Misty very happy. Nick was still giving me the stink eye. But I thought we might be on to something. At that time, I just didn't want to discuss the logistics of a half dozen flimsy canoes attacking a paddlewheel steamboat full of well-armed killers in the middle of a crocodile and piranha-filled river.

****

We dragged six boats to the river's edge. I put Misty up front with me in the back of one. Nick rode up front with Crash in the back of another. The next three boats carried two vaqueros each with Paulo paddling solo with the supplies in the last. We pushed off into the river, disturbing many water bugs, mosquitos, gnats and a few birds that were dining on them.

We stayed close to the northern shore as we got our paddling in sync. Crash almost had to use his paddle on Nick's head to keep him from causing the boat to go in a circle. It didn't take long until we were moving along quite well, like a hillbilly version of the Harvard—Yale Regatta rowing teams.

I looked at beautiful Misty, paddling along in front of me and felt like she should have been facing me with a dozen roses in her lap; and I, wearing a boater instead of Stetson, should have been singing a love song while accompanying myself on a ukulele. My mind returned to reality as a crocodile splashed into the water, causing us to bob on its wake. Oh, well. I can't play the ukulele anyway, or sing either, for that matter.

Looking out over the river at the endless jungle that followed both banks, I felt relaxed. Every now and then, we would all stop paddling and just ride the current, using the back paddle as a rudder. "I think I could get to like this," I said, while Nick frowned at me from his boat.

"What's that?" Misty pointed ahead at what looked like a massive blue cloud floating along in front of us. When we got closer, I smiled. "It's only a bunch of dragonflies," I said. "Pretty ones, at that."

"I'm not sure what they're doing," Crash offered, "but some of them are flying united."

"Then you do know what they are doing."

Misty chuckled, which made me smile, until the splashing started. Apparently, some of the river's fish were actually leaping out of the water to enjoy a communal dragonfly brunch. We were right in the middle of the cloud when the fish behavior began getting out of hand. They were leaping around and even over us to get their teeth on the big blue flying refreshments.

"I think some of those fish have red bellies!" an agitated Nick Danby yelled, and started swinging his paddle like he thought he was the Sultan of Swat, with fish.

"Do not panic, senhor," Paulo said. "Stay calm, and if they drop in your boat, pick them up by the tail so they don't bite you, and toss them back."

Nick's eyes were wide and angry as he stopped batting and yelled, "Curly! This is your fault!"

"How is it my fault," I quietly asked the frantic chauffeur.

"I don't know. But it is!"

It didn't take long for us to get through the blue cloud and the feeding fish. Nick and Crash were the last to exit the dragonfly gathering in that they had paddled in a circle a few times until the chauffeur calmed down.

The quiet time on the river gave me an opportunity to think. And although I found it difficult to take my thoughts away from my shapely shipmate, I was able to relax and ponder our situation a little. I came to the conclusion that a lot of things didn't add up.

We had escaped Rancho Grandé. And, I was pretty sure that, by then, our troops were making the grounds safe again for normal-sized insects and surviving cattle. We had rescued Misty and the real Dom Sebastian while killing the fake Dom and his Moslem minions. And, thanks to quick-draw Misty, the mad Dr. LaFond was toast. Hopefully, our two planeloads of party refugees were able to reach safety and Donovan got a chance to schedule a rescue aircraft to meet us in Manaus.

So what in the heck did we walk into at the native village? The brass left strewn around the murder site told us the native villagers had no chance against such firepower. There were plenty of .30 caliber shell casings showing some of the attackers were using rifles. But the majority of the brass was from .45 caliber ammunition. I surmised from the separate piles that at least four of the shooters were armed with Thompson submachine guns.

The slaughter probably didn't take very long. It had been carried out with almost military-like precision. Yet, there were no revolutionary movements going on in Brazil at that time. In fact, the country's long-time leader, President Vargas, had a fairly close relationship with the Roosevelt administration. So if we had stumbled into a new war, I was at a loss in figuring out the identity of my enemy.

I estimated the river's current speed at ranging between eight and four miles per hour. That added up to a total of two or three more days to reach Manaus, if we continued without stopping. Of course, we would have to stop now and then to rest, eat beans, boil water to drink and, probably, sleep. That expanded my estimation to up to six days.

And then there was the steamboat containing submachine gun-totin', maniacal killers somewhere between where we were and our destination. Like the man said, "Nothing can go wrong."

****

We were well into the warm afternoon when I noticed Nick fidgeting. His eyes were bulging and he seemed to be motioning some sort of signals to me. Well, I've already discussed my lack of ability at deciphering body language. So it took me a few minutes to realize, he had to pee, but was afraid of standing up in the boat.

"Let's go to the shore," I said. "We all need a nature break."

We paddled to a somewhat safe-looking shore, lacking in thick shrubs and carnivorous beasts. Dragging our boats out of the water, we quickly separated for trips to a variety of Amazon jungle restrooms, complete with tree-trunk privacy and convenient leaves.

I gathered kindling and started a small fire to heat our beans and, later, boil our water in the bean cans. Misty pulled up a small log and sat down next to me in front of the fire.

"How're we doin', Curly?"

"So far, so good."

"Do you think we have a chance of catching up with that riverboat?"

I thought a moment. "If I was right about their firewood situation and they have taken the time to cut their own, then maybe."

"But if we stay here and camp, we'd never catch them."

"That's true. So we'll just have a bite of beans, drink some canteen water and take a two-hour rest before getting back on the way."

"I'm not hungry," she said, leaning up against me. "I think I'll just take a quick nap."

"Have a drink first. I'll refill the canteen with boiled water before we leave."

I chose one of the blankets, folded it and placed it on the ground for her to use as a pillow. Nick and Crash joined me in the bean cooking. Nick's bayonet came in handy, again, to open the cans. We all used flat sticks as spoons.

"Too bad we don't have something other than beans and crackers," Nick said, "especially for you, Curly."

"Huh?"

"I mean, a few miles down the river, both you and Misty may be reconsidering your choice to have beans."

"Thanks, buddy. Always thinkin' of me."

"I overheard you talkin' about catching up with the riverboat," Crash said. "Why would we want to do that?"

"I want to know who killed everyone in that village," I said. "And I'd like to get even."

"And how do we attack and conquer a big boat full of machine-gun carrying maniacs with our little canoes and small arms?"

"Very carefully," I said, while folding a leaf and using it to grip the lid of a can of hot beans. "We'll figure something out."

"Oh," Nick said. "That explains it. Thank you, Curly. I feel so much better now."

I waved for the vaqueros to join us. They smiled, brought more bean cans and sat. I picked up Misty's canteen and took a long swig.

"Drink up, guys. Then we'll boil up some water and refill all of the canteens."

The vaqueros talked among themselves. Paulo joined in both their discussions and ours. His language skills had become extremely valuable, and our translated discussions had allowed all of us to become closer.

After two hours, I awakened those who were smart enough to nap. Crash repacked our supplies and placed them back in the boats while Nick stomped out the remains of the campfire and made sure we buried our trash. One thing about a hot, damp jungle, trash becomes compost quickly. Even tin cans will be reduced to a handful of rust within a few months.

"Thanks for watching over me," Misty said. "It's a shame we don't have more time and a little more privacy."

"Watching over you is a privilege," I whispered, embracing her warmly. "And if we get out of this alive, I'll make sure we get the time and the privacy."

Back on the water, we progressed slowly eastward while watching our shadows growing longer. Dusk joined a slight breeze in cooling us off and cautioning us to be on guard. My mind suddenly remembered Nick's mean warning that I might regret having eaten a full can of beans. I heard a slight rumble coming up from my digestive tract and I looked over at the smartass chauffeur as if it were his fault. Then the smell hit me.

No, it wasn't me that I smelled. It was the slight essence of burning wood. Looking into the early evening sky, I could see a light cloud of soot floating above us.

"To the shore!" I whispered.

The others must have noticed the smoke at the same time. We all quietly paddled to the riverbank, pulled our boats out of the water and made sure our weapons were either in our holsters or our hands.

"The riverboat has to be just around the bend," I said in my best library voice. "It's not dark enough yet to advance on it in our canoes."

"So we should just wait a while, then follow it in the dark?" Misty asked.

"I don't think the paddle wheeler is moving. It wasn't in the middle of the river, which means it's probably anchored near the shore to gather fuel for the furnace."

"Let's go take a looksee," Misty said.

"No. You stay here. No fires. No noise. Paulo and I will, quietly, patrol ahead and learn what we can."

It was a slow slog through the thick foliage as we tried not to make a sound. And we were successful except for two low noises I have to blame on the beans. After fifteen minutes of stealthy strides, we slowed and took prone positions behind a large tree trunk. From our elevated position, we saw an approximately sixty-foot sternwheeler scow pushed up into branches that overhung the riverside.

A steady trickle of smoke escaped the single stack on top of the ancient vessel. The steamboat had probably been an amazing piece of technology late in the last century. But it had obviously survived some hard years. Much of the siding wood was warped with peeling blisters of ancient paint hanging off while areas of originally ornate railings had been broken, some completely missing. I had a hard time picturing Charles Winninger as Cap'n Andy welcoming passengers aboard, and I didn't think even Allan Jones could carry a tune on that old scow.

The sun was down and a centrally positioned fire crackled in a work area close to the riverbank. It looked like the harvesters were burning the branches that were either too thick or too spindly to be used for the boat's furnace. But the blazing wood illuminated the scurrying human beings in a quality of light that Lon Chaney's Phantom would have appreciated.

A not-so-trustworthy gangplank precariously spanned from the riverboat, close to the overhanging branches, over to the shore. A goodly amount of firewood was stacked on the bank next to the plank. There were six men that I could see, with machetes and axes, ripping into some dry, downed tree branches, while three men with rifles kept a close watch on them.

Paulo tapped me on the shoulder and motioned to my left. I turned and saw the firelight reflecting on one side of a man armed with a Thompson submachine gun seated some twenty yards farther into the jungle. I noticed two more chopper-bearing guards farther away, behind the firewood gatherers.

All of the armed men were wearing dark green shirts, pants and caps. The men cutting wood wore faded white and gray work clothes. I guessed they were probably riverboat crewmembers being kept alive to gather wood and operate the boat. All of the work crew had dark weathered skin from years of laboring in the sun. The armed men were very white, some with bright blond hair.

From the brass we saw at the river massacre, I figured there were at least four Thompsons. Some of the bad guys had to still be on the boat.

"Let's get a little closer and see if we can hear anything important," I whispered to Paulo. "I doubt they will have to cut much more firewood, but they still need to load it aboard."

We low-crawled a bit closer to the operation and, with leaves and sticks on top of us, listened. It didn't take long to hear what we needed to know.

"Those thugs are speaking German," Paulo whispered.

My eyes went wide with realization as I saw a tall, sandy haired man wearing khaki pants, riding boots and a dark blue shirt walk down the gangplank to inspect the firewood. He blew smoke from a cigarette through his pencil-thin mustache and smiled like a condor at dinnertime. It was Maria's horse trainer, Dante, with a Luger on his hip and a pretentious swagger stick in his hand.

"Recognize that pile of shit?" I whispered.

"Yes, senhor. It's the horse trainer who spent all of his time away from the stables."

"My guess is Herr Dante had other duties. And by his expression, I don't think it will be long before they load all that wood. Let's go get the others. Time is running out."

We quietly backed out of the area and hurried toward our friends. I knew our window of opportunity was closing. If we were going to get even with those killers, we had to do it before they finished loading the firewood on the boat – and we would need the vaqueros and all of the firepower we possessed.

"Germans!" I thought. "The fake Dom Sebastian admitted he and his Moslem drug runners were being funded by both National Socialists and Soviet Socialists. It makes sense. Kitchen helpers/pilots Hans and Fritz were planning on flying the DC-3 out with opium, G-719 poison, and all of their collaborators, including the Moslems and these Nazis.

"But why hadn't we seen any of the goose-steppers at the ranch?" my brain continued to question itself. "The Germans had to have been housed at the former barracks near the runway. Once Hans and Fritz were taken captive, they probably burned their building and headed for the village with knowledge of the riverboat deliveries."

My head was splitting by the time we reached our friends. I quickly explained the situation to Crash, Nick and Misty while Paulo did the same for his vaqueros. Then, I laid out the basics of a plan for all of us.

With an intense sense of purpose, we returned to the site of the fuel harvesting. The three riflemen were standing close to the gangplank while the white-shirted workers hauled armloads of firewood onto the riverboat. The three machine-gun guards were still in their same locations overlooking the labor. Smoke from the stack had increased in volume, telling me the steamboat was preparing to leave.

I positioned the vaqueros in a wider perimeter around the Thompson carrying guards, and organized it so two vaqueros would have their rifles aimed at each one of the three machine gunners. I borrowed Nick's bayonet and placed him, Crash and Misty in position to take out the three riflemen just as soon as they heard the first shot fired.

Paulo and I targeted the two closest machine gunners for an attempted silent removal. We quietly low-crawled toward our prey, knowing that if we could kill both of them without firing a shot, we would be able to take their firepower for our own assault.

With the bayonet in my hand, I slithered up to within a yard of the unsuspecting German killer. My teeth were clenched, as I crouched and prepared to dive at the man for a quick kill. My body froze in place and tightened up like a rock when his head began to turn in my direction. Then the riverboat whistle blew twice, to let the gunners know it was time to leave.

Time to leave is right, as he straightened up and looked back at the riverboat just in time for my blade to rip into the back of his neck and come out the front. He arched his back, gurgled and dropped his weapon. The second guard screamed as Paulo's machete took off his arm and then returned for his head. The third Thompson carrying Hun lifted his gun, only to receive several .30 caliber slugs in his belly.

The three riflemen dropped at the same time as Nick, Misty and Crash opened fire, scoring bullseyes. The workers dived for cover. One of them slipped into the water with a load of firewood, only to come running out of the river with one fish chomped onto his rear. Lucky for him he was a fast mover and that there was only one hungry piranha near the plank that was quick enough to take a bite.

The vaqueros and I ran screaming like rebels toward the riverboat. I had directed Crash, Nick and Misty to stay in position and snipe any enemy they might see while the rest of us engaged in a full-scale assault. Paulo, another vaquero and I had commandeered the amazing Thompsons and were chewing up pieces of the ragged riverboat, with special effort not to destroy the pilothouse or puncture any part of the craft's flat-bottomed hull.

Someone was firing a bolt-action rifle from the stern, just above the wheel. I concentrated my fire on the area, and the shooting stopped. Then I noticed the tall man standing next to the pilothouse with a Thompson in his hand. It was Dante, blasting away at us in a fine impersonation of Paul Muni from "Scarface." He shredded the ground in front of our advance, leaving a trail of bullet scars all the way across two vaqueros, who dropped to the ground grasping their ripped flesh as they died.

It was Dante, blasting away at us in a fine impersonation of Paul Muni from "Scarface."

I heard Paulo yell something that didn't need interpreting as he and I focused our fire on the Nazi killer. The horse trainer slammed up against the pilothouse, then slid downward onto his butt, leaving a red slimy trail on the wall. His eyes rolled up into his head and I wished Dante an unpleasant trip to his forever inferno.

All shooting stopped as we let the silence wash over us. I hollered for Misty and Nick to stay put and keep a sniper's eye on our surroundings. Crash jogged down toward our position near the plank. Paulo ran to his downed men, then stood back up to join me in advancing toward the slightly damaged Rio Amazon sternwheeler. Two of the vaqueros questioned the workers in Portuguese while the other two gathered rifles and ammunition from the dead.

"These men were captured by the killers and forced to operate the boat," Paulo said.

"Are any of them wounded?"

"Only one. He was bitten by a piranha, but he'll be fine."

"Are there any more bad guys?"

"All of the Nazis are dead, except for that one."

He pointed to the stern where I had blasted at the sniper. A dark human form looked out from behind a broken rail and laughed. It seemed to be standing on its knees, leaning against the railing. I ran forward with my Thompson ready to shred the enemy, only to almost fall off the boat when I saw the killer.

Kneeling in front of me, dressed in black boots, jodhpurs and blouse with a bloodstained orange scarf draped across her shoulder was our former hostess, Maria. Her left arm was wounded nicely with just the hint of a bone sticking out above the elbow. A bullet had also done a number on her lower right ribs, soaking her blouse with Nazi blood. And her once beautiful face had added what looked like a perfect Heidelberg dueling saber slash.

"Delighted to see you again, Curly," she wheezed. "You cowboys are a real pain in the ass."

"And you seem to have done pretty well for yourself, up until now, for a former chorus girl from Rio."

She laughed. "You've been listening to the rug maker. That tool and his Moslem followers over valued themselves."

Nick and Misty joined us on the boat.

"So you and your 'horse trainer' were his financiers?" I asked.

"I, and my soldiers, oversaw the complete operation for Germany's efforts in this part of the world – and it was very productive and lucrative until you came along. As for our Moslem assistants, we, Hitler's National Socialists, have uses for lots of people – brown, black, white, poor, rich, Christians, Moslems, Jews. A few are allowed to join us, for a bit, while others are designed to be useful until we can wipe them out of our way."

One of the vaqueros came up to Paulo and spoke to him in Portuguese.

"The riverboat workers said they were taken captive at the village, as this evil woman led the annihilation of the native people," Paulo interpreted.

"No great loss," she said, with boredom in her voice like an Aryan Marie Antoinette. "They had no skills of value to the Fatherland."

I held up my hand, as I saw Misty advance toward the witch with her pistol in her hand. She paused, glowering at the former Rancho Grandé hostess with death in her eyes.

"And your name probably isn't really Maria," I continued

"Maria will do, for a headstone," Misty said.

"Don't be so optimistic, Misty. I believe we can patch her up enough to reach Manaus," I said. Then I looked down at the wounded butcher. "We have a couple of G-men friends who would be delighted to converse with you, Maria."

"Ah, but you don't understand," she smiled like a rattlesnake. "Germany and the United States are not at war, yet. Brazil has declared its neutrality. And I have several friends from home and our embassy waiting to greet me in Manaus. You wouldn't want to start a war by trying to kidnap an innocent German citizen, would you? Perhaps your friends and mine could have a discussion at a later time."

"Crash, keep your rifle aimed at this atrocity," I said. "Paulo, let's finish up here and get this boat movin'."

I went ashore and helped the vaqueros bury their slain comrades. Then we tossed the dead Nazis into the river in our efforts to help feed poor and undernourished piranhas and crocodiles. I just hoped the river critters wouldn't become ill.

Two of the rescued workers went to the wheelhouse while the other four scattered over the riverboat, preparing to get us moving.

I returned to where Crash stood over Maria.

"What do you want to do with this thing?" he asked.

"Well, she's bleeding for one," I said. "So let's get her away from the stern wheel so, if she falls, she won't screw up the big paddle."

"Where do you want her?"

"Over by the side railing, where she can't hurt anything."

She screamed in pain as we grabbed her by the arms, dragged her to the port side and propped her back up on her knees.

"I thought you said you could patch me up so we can get to Manaus," she whined.

"I told you that before you mentioned your friends from the embassy," I said. "Right now, I can't think of any reason to keep you alive."

"But you Americans don't kill without a reason. Killing me now would be murder, an act of war!"

"You could call it that, but when we arrive at Manaus, no one will know you were ever here. And, just like those villagers being of no use to your Fatherland, you are no longer any use to – us."

Crash placed the barrel of his rifle on the Nazi's forehead. "Let me do it, Curly. That might help erase the vision of that bloody cradle from my memory."

Maria screamed and clasped her hands together to beg. "You can't shoot me! That's uncivilized!"

"Oh, we're not going to shoot you, Maria," I smiled. "I wouldn't want you to think I was uncivilized. In fact, we're going to let you confer with some of your like-minded friends."

Her eyes went from confused to complete terror as I lifted my foot and, with the bottom of my boot, shoved her through the broken railing and into the beautiful Amazon River where her friends arrived immediately to chew over good times.

CHAPTER 12. THE LONG TRAIL HOME

It didn't take long for the riverboat crew and vaqueros to finish loading the firewood, stoke up the furnace and get the paddles rollin'. Lucas took to the wheel in the pilothouse as our captain. Antonio assisted as a new executive officer. Marcos, Luiz, Gabriel and Leonardo went below to keep the furnaces stoked and the steam engine pumping along.

The rest of us found places on the boat to rest and ponder our progress. Some of the vaqueros dropped directly to the deck and fell asleep. Misty and I found a nice little corner in a cargo hold containing stacked bales of cotton that gave us a little privacy to snuggle.

"Well," I said, while looking around at our makeshift stateroom. "It ain't the Waldorf."

"Don't be silly, Curly. This place has nothing to do with a salad."

"You've been listening to too many Burns and Allen shows."

She kissed me on the nose and smiled. "I'd love to listen to one of their shows right now."

"I could think of other things I'd rather do," I whispered, while nibbling on her ear.

"Me too," she giggled, "but I think we should get a little sleep right now. Anything else might wake the baby."

"Huh? What baby?"

"The one on the other side of that bale."

"Hi, Curly," Nick's voice lifted over the cotton like an ice shower. "I'm right next door."

"G'night, Nick," Misty said, while closing her eyes and leaning in close.

"G'night, Misty," Nick said.

"G'night, Misty, Nick, Curly," Corrigan's voice sounded from behind another bale.

I cursed, pulled my hat over my face and fell asleep.

****

Over the next two and a half days we caught up on our sleep and learned a lot about riverboats. Nick became very friendly with the crew and spent some time actually at the wheel, with Lucas standing next to him. He also went below, stoked the furnace, got to understand the pressure gauges on the steam engine and learned that Brazilians were better poker players than he was.

Nick was extremely close to Leonardo, whom he called Leo, after he shared a hidden stash of Mexican beer with the chauffeur. Corrigan found a pencil and some paper, which he used to jot down Range Busters scenarios for his Monogram series. Misty and I just hung out on deck pretending we were cruising from Miami to Havana on the S.S. Florida, minus the deck chairs, fruity drinks and gourmet meals.

Lucky for us, there was a poor man's galley where we could make coffee and heat up cans of soup. We decided to skip the beans. In fact, thanks to our previously limited cuisine, I also rethought my desire to take Misty for lunch at Barney's Beanery.

Another luxury we were pleased with was the below deck latrine. (I know sailors will correct me that the proper term would be "head," but I was Army. So it's "latrine.") It was a two-seater with a liberal supply of Portuguese language fan magazines. On my first visit, I relished the use of a few pages from an MGM flack article and photos about Lew Ayres in the Dr. Kildare series. (I never did like that guy.)

Thanks to the fact that there were so many of us aboard, Misty and I spent most of our waking hours talking. Talking. Talking. Talking. Geesh!

"Do you think that any G-719 survived the fires?" she asked while we strolled along the deck.

"God, I hope not!"

"If there were a way to make it safe to use on crops, it could certainly help stem the problem of hunger in the world."

"That's a big 'if,'" I replied. "Corn grows pretty well just about everywhere. Nature has this one, without humans screwing things up. We don't need to play Frankenstein with the world's food supply."

We held hands and talked about movies, books and our jobs. I knew I couldn't wait to get back to the peace and calm of flacking for Republic's B-westerns in good old, common sense, stable Hollywood. And, I had hoped Misty would want to join me, and my delightful kitten Spade, in my little Culver City bungalow. No such luck. She told me she couldn't wait to get back to the insane behavior and vacuous partisan politics of Washington, D.C. Of course, those were all my words, not hers.

****

It was early morning when we got near Manaus. Everything was quiet and calm, except that Nick was at the wheel and blowing the whistle at every small boat that got near us. Manaus was a thriving frontier town with a lot of river traffic and what looked to be a busy river port. I yelled in for Nick to turn the wheel over to Lucas but, as usual, he ignored me. And he did an almost good job of parking the Rio Amazon, except for minimal damage to the dock and a couple of other boats.

Once ropes were attached and everyone stopped yelling at us, we all exited the sternwheeler and sauntered across the newly shattered boardwalk toward a wooden terminal where three uniformed men stood waiting for us. Of course, we were all heavily armed. I just had my Luger resting in my shoulder holster. But the Thompson submachine gun I carried in my right hand did look a little suspicious. All of us had pistols, some carried Springfield rifles as well, and Paulo and another vaquero sported their captured Thompsons. The Brazilian cowboys kept their grenades hidden in their clothing.

Paulo walked to the Brazilian Army officer who stood in our path and had an extensive conversation with the man. He then walked back to us and said, "My country has been waiting for you."

I swallowed and waited for the other guillotine blade to drop.

"Agent Slate has arranged transportation for you to the airfield where a B-18 awaits your arrival," Paulo said. "My uniformed countrymen will escort you. My friends and I will stay here until we can find work on another ranch. The riverboat crew will also await a new assignment."

"So, they're not going to line us up and shoot us?" I asked.

"No. But you might want to take their offer up quickly, before anyone starts talking about missing Nazis, giant bugs or that massacred village."

"That's wonderful," I said, as I stepped forward and shook the officer's hand. Two enlisted men stood by his side, smiling.

"There is one thing," Paulo said. "Actually two. He's going to confiscate all of the Thompson submachine guns."

"No problem. What's the second thing?"

"All three of the soldiers would like Mr. Corrigan's autograph."

Crash stepped forward with a big Mesquiteer grin and did the honors. We all shook hands, slapped backs and smiled. (Who said we couldn't be diplomatic?) I looked out the back door of the office and could see Donovan Slate waiting with Wagner and Long next to a bus. Misty, Nick, Crash and I said our goodbyes to the riverboat crew and then, with handshakes and a few hugs, to our lifesaving vaqueros.

The four of us left the building and walked directly to the bus and Donovan, Wagner and Long. Standing not too far away were five rather pretentious looking men in gray suits leaning against another bus with a swastika on it.

"Get inside, quickly," Donovan said.

We climbed in the bus to find three more armed Brazilian soldiers already seated.

"They're here for our protection," Donovan said, as Long started the bus and hit the road.

The soldiers moved closer to Corrigan and the big ham smiled and, with a borrowed pencil, made three new friends with the uniformed fans.

"The Nazis are gonna be disappointed," I said. "Maybe their people will be on the next boat."

Slate didn't say a word.

"The B-18 will start its propellers turning as soon as they see this bus coming," Wagner said. "We'll debrief in the air."

Misty and I snuggled together for the fifteen-minute ride to the airport.

"We've got another long ride to get back to the states," she said. "You think maybe we'll get some privacy soon?"

I looked around at the soldiers, the three G-men, Crash and Nick and grumbled.

As we drove down into the valley to the airfield, I could see the B-18 warming up and positioning itself for a quick takeoff. Right next to it was a new beautiful twin-engine Beechcraft C-45, also warming up.

"Hey, Donovan," I said. "That C-45 holds nine passengers and travels up to 225 miles per hour. Can we go home in that?"

"It would be nice, but no," he answered. "That plane is here for a very special passenger."

"Well, whoever that is, is lucky," Nick said. "That B-18 is gonna be another bumpy two-day flight."

"Would you rather go by steamboat?"

"No."

"Then get off the bus," Slate ordered as we stopped near the two airplanes. "Let's go."

We hopped out of the bus and ran toward the B-18.

"Curly, lead the way!"

I hurried up the steps and into the big plane, with Nick and Crash right behind me. Then Wagner and Donovan followed. Wagner slammed the door closed and the plane started moving.

"Hey! Stop! Misty's not here!" I yelled.

"I know," Donovan said. "She and agent Long are headed to D.C. on the C-45."

I looked out the window to see the Beechcraft race down the runway and lift into the air. Then the B-18 engines roared and our plane began its awkward rumble toward liftoff. I stared at Donovan Slate with an expression that, if it were as powerful as it was angry, that devious G-man would have been covered in poison darts.

"President Roosevelt wants Arlene Mistevin back in Washington immediately," Slate said. "You, however, can make your report to me on the way back to Los Angeles."

At that time, I didn't have to say anything to communicate my thoughts.

Wagner pointed to a bag near my feet. "Hey, I got you guys

some new comics."

That earned him a full share of stink eye.

"So, what were the Nazis waiting for?" Donovan asked.

Crash looked at me and smiled. "Curly. You and Misty will see each other again. You know it and I know it. And the next time you won't be surrounded by the rest of us."

I started to calm down, sort of. Then Slate pulled a tarp off of a case of, surprisingly cool, bottles of beer. That put a smile on the chauffeur's face. Crash winked as he grabbed a beer. I took a bottle, but I didn't smile.

Two bottles later, Nick was regaling the G-men with a slightly exaggerated account of our travels. Eventually, I had to step in to accurately relate the situation at the native village, as well as to make sure that all of the Nazis' deaths were unquestionably necessary and in defense of our own lives.

Donovan listened without remarking. Then he filled us in on the escape flights from Rancho Grandé. They had followed my advice and burned the opium and G-719 around the runway just before they took off.

"What happened to Hans and Fritz?" I asked.

"As we figured, we didn't have enough room for them in our planes," he said. "So we left them tied up in the hangar. I really don't know whether they were still there when our forces landed, or if they escaped or were eaten by giant mosquitoes wearing black capes. Maybe I'll find out when the mop up is concluded."

"And everyone else was flown to safety?" Crash asked.

"Yes," Slate answered. "We flew into Lima where all factions were able to arrange for transportation to their home countries. Then we immediately came to get you."

I walked to the back of the plane and visited one of the lidded buckets. When I got back, I snatched another beer and one of Wagner's new comic books, an issue of *Silver Streak*, featuring the Daredevil and one of my favorite villains, the Claw. I was beginning to relax, knowing it was going to be a long flight and I couldn't stay angry the whole trip. Then I thought about Misty and began to rethink how long I could stay angry.

Crash was laughing and giving Nick a hard time about his clumsy attempt to dock the riverboat, which also brought a small smile to my lips. Danby started to reach for an issue of *Captain*

America Comics when he looked up and froze. We all went silent as our pilot, Bob, left the cockpit and started to walk past us toward the lidded buckets.

"What the hell, Bob?" I spat.

"Oh, hi guys. How's it goin'?"

"What happened to the little tube and funnel you have up front?"

"I can't use that with a copilot sitting next to me," he answered.

I relaxed and a rather loud sigh of relief came from Nick after learning we had a copilot flying the plane.

"Yeah, we've got our own case, or two, of beer up there," he said. "So we'll both be traipsing back here now and then."

Bob continued his trek to the buckets as Nick and I sat back and started reading our comic books. Something didn't seem right, the hair on my neck told me. Simultaneously the chauffeur and I lifted our heads and looked at each other with wide eyes. We glanced at Donovan, who was whistling and fiddling with his cigar clipper.

Both of us jumped to our feet and ran to the cockpit. There, sitting in the copilot seat was our worst nightmare with a beer balanced on his knee, one hand on the yoke and the other thumbing through a manual on how to fly a B-18. We both turned and ran back into the cargo bay.

"Holy shit!" Nick hollered. "Hoot's flying this plane!"

"Where are the parachutes?" I yelled.

FADE TO BLACK

Made in the USA
Coppell, TX
12 December 2022

89026657R00090